Always and Forever Friends

C.S. ADLER has written some of her twenty-eight published books for children and young adults in Wellfleet, Massachusetts, where she spends summers walking the beaches and working the computer. The rest of her novels are written in Niskayuna, a town next to Schenectady, New York. At one time Carol Adler taught English in middle school in Niskayuna, and she and her husband raised their three sons there.

Many of Adler's books have also been published in Japan, Germany, England, Denmark, and Austria. She won the Golden Kite Award and the William Allen White Award for her first book, *The Magic of the Glits*, and has since won other literary prizes. Her books have often been on the Children's Choices list and have been chosen for many state lists.

Always and Forever Friends

C.S. Adler

AN AVON CAMELOT BOOK

AVON BOOKS
A division of
The Hearst Corporation
1350 Avenue of the Americas
New York, New York 10019

"A Clarion Book"
Copyright © 1988 by C. S. Adler
Published by arrangement with Houghton Mifflin Company
Library of Congress Catalog Card Number: 87-18230
ISBN: 0-380-70687-3
RL: 4.8

First Avon Camelot Printing: February 1990

CAMELOT TRADEMARK REG. U.S. PAT. OFF. AND IN OTHER COUNTRIES, MARCA
REGISTRADA, HECHO EN U.S.A.

Printed in the U.S.A.

OPM   10   9   8   7

For Phil Sadler,
In appreciation for his decades of devotion to introducing children to children's book authors and those authors to each other.

Contents

Always and Forever Friends

Wanted, a Best Friend

With Meg gone, Wendy felt as lonely as she had on her first day in Miss Pinelli's brightly decorated sixth grade classroom. True, the faces around her were now attached to familiar names and personalities, but none of them was attached to her. They revolved in closed orbits of twos or threes or fours while she sat alone trying not to look at Meg's vacant desk. She and Meg had paired up immediately last September, so that Wendy hadn't missed her old friends in Brooklyn too painfully, and Mother had been proud of Wendy's easy adjustment to the first new school in her life. Now the lilacs on Miss Pinelli's desk were scenting the air with spring, but instead of feeling like a balloon on a string, Wendy felt punctured. Even spring was flat without a best friend.

She shut her eyes and concentrated on wishing for a new girl to walk through the door. Miss Pinelli would call for a volunteer buddy and Wendy would raise her hand. The new girl would be a little scared and Wendy would comfort her and explain how things worked here. Any minute the door would open and. . . .

"Before we begin our new unit," Miss Pinelli was saying in the fluty voice that fit with her long narrow body and skinny legs, "we'll share a few of the compositions on human relationships you did last week. Some of these were really special."

The first composition was about a football team. One of the boys wrote it, Wendy figured. The boys in her class were mostly jocks who spent their free time huddled together talking sports and acting as if girls didn't exist. Except for Jeremy. Well, Jeremy was absent today which was why the class was so peaceful. Probably he hadn't written anything anyway.

Miss Pinelli perched on her desk and began the second composition entitled, "My little brother." Laughter greeted the humor in it, and Wendy wished she'd thought to write about her stepbrothers, Chick and Eric, instead of pouring her heart out about Meg and friendship. If Miss Pinelli read her piece to the class, Wendy would die of embarrassment. Lucky her writing was never good enough to be shared.

Judging by the knowing glances Marcy was getting from her friends over there in the front rows by the windows, she must have written, "My Little Brother." Wendy watched Marcy wistfully. Nobody in the class was sweeter or more friendly than Marcy, and she was so pretty. She looked like a junior-sized fashion model. Today she and her best friend Sarah wore matching pink bracelets. The other two in their group, Becky and Jill, were just average, but they dressed fashionably too. When the four of them put their heads together and laughed about something, Wendy longed more than ever to be one of a group, the way it had been for her in Brooklyn.

None of the other girls in class seemed to have fun. The worst was the other Sarah who whined and had allergies. Hee Chung and Dorothy were buddies. Hee Chung never spoke above a whisper, and tiny Dorothy looked as if she were escaping down a mousehole when she and Hee Chung left for their private music lessons. Barbara, the brain, sometimes hung out with them when she took time off from being teacher's pet.

Then there was Honor. Honor was the girl Wendy admired most besides Marcy. Miss Pinelli was reading Honor's composition now. No question it was hers. Who else would write about a black lady politician in Texas named Barbara Jordan in such an adult-sounding style? Wendy smiled across the aisle at Honor in appreciation of the composition, but Honor was looking straight ahead. Her ruff of springy black hair had a paper clip stuck in it, probably by the boy behind her. Wendy would have reached over to pull it out except with Honor she wouldn't dare take personal liberties. Instead she wrote a note—"Paper clip in hair."—and slipped it onto Honor's desk. Honor nodded and felt for the wire, removing it with the calm dignity with which she did everything. She was the only one who hadn't come to the Halloween party Wendy had given for the class last October. She'd said her grandmother was taking her out someplace.

Wendy had had such hopes that the party would expand her social circle. Marcy and her friends had come, and afterward Marcy *had* promised to invite Wendy to her house, but she hadn't yet. Meg used to say Marcy was a snob. What Wendy thought was that Marcy might not have room in her life for more friends unless they were special, and Wendy knew she wasn't special, just a plain all-around ordinary nice kid.

"Friendship is a sharing of fun and also the good and bad things that happen to you," Miss Pinelli read.

Was that her composition? It couldn't be. Wendy sucked in air and felt her cheeks get hot.

". . . like when my cat, Tinkerboy, was gone for a week and I thought I'd lost him forever, Meg helped me stick up signs where people might see, and she even found a kitten if I needed a new one," Miss Pinelli read with feeling. "Then Tinkerboy showed up and Meg was as glad as I was. She bought him a toy ball with a bell inside. Meg roots for me and I root for her.

". . . Even though Meg and I aren't related, we're alike. We both have the same color hair and both our birthdays are in May, and we like talking on the phone every night and never run out of things to say. If I'm watching a TV program, I always know she'll be watching the same one.

". . . Nothing's more important than a best friend who's always and forever, except having parents you love."

Wendy could feel them all looking at her, even though she kept her eyes fixed on the death's head inked onto her desk. If she'd only had sense enough not to use Meg's name! They'd all seen her make a fool of herself the day Meg left for Thailand and now this. They were going to think she was as weird as Jeremy who said what he felt right out without even noticing people's reactions.

Miss Pinelli put the compositions aside and began explaining the new project. They were all to work in groups collecting research on the history of mankind. Each group could decide how to do their research, whether to use the library and filmstrips or go to the Hall of Man at the museum. Every group would fill out a set of work sheets and be evaluated on how completely and well they'd researched. "Best of all," Miss Pinelli finished triumphantly, "I'm going to let you choose who you want to work with. This late in the year you know each other well enough. Of course, anyone who goofs off will shortly find him or herself working alone."

Even after Miss Pinelli told them to group and choose a leader, Wendy sat stiff and still in her embarrassment over the composition. She had ten minutes to get through until math. Much as she hated math, she wished it would hurry and come.

Next to her, Honor shoveled herself out of her desk

and moved to the front of the room where Barbara was beckoning her to join Dorothy and Hee Chung. Barbara would only work with the best students like Honor and Hee Chung. Marcy's group was already relaxed together and chattering. Bruce and Jason walked past Wendy. Like a matched pair of horses, they did everything together. They'd probably get stuck with Jeremy when he came back because they were too quiet and steady for him to disrupt. The other Sarah didn't have anyone to work with. Oh, oh, Wendy thought, and sighed. Miss Pinelli was busy telling the rest of the boys that nine was too large a group, and they had to split it in half or thirds. She left them arguing and headed like a quick, dark bird toward Wendy.

"Wendy, the other Sarah asked if she could work alone because she's going to be out so much for her allergy shots."

Wendy managed a smile. "Okay, I'll work alone too."

"No, no." Miss Pinelli looked around. "Who would you *like* to work with?"

"Well—" Wendy's eyes strayed longingly to Marcy's group, but she cringed when Miss Pinelli patted her on the shoulder and flew off in that direction. Miss Pinelli leaned on Sarah's desk and said something to Marcy. Awful, Wendy thought, and wished she were invisible.

Marcy smiled up at Miss Pinelli, but the other three glared at Wendy over their shoulders. Wendy looked away and pretended to drop a pencil and poke around under her desk for it. Miss Pinelli returned and said, "Okay, you'll be with Marcy and Sarah then." She smiled at Wendy and Wendy thanked her. Miss Pinelli meant well. At the beginning of the term she'd seemed very strict and mean, but though she *was* strict, she'd turned out to be a very good teacher.

Quietly Wendy joined the group at the window by sitting on the corner of an unused desk near them to listen. "So we're going to do the museum and we need to know when everybody's free to go." Marcy turned to Wendy.

"I'm free anytime," Wendy said.

"Well, can your mother drive?"

"Maybe. I'll ask her. Just tell me when."

"*My* mother doesn't mind driving, and we've got a new station wagon with an extra seat in the back that we can all fit in," Sarah said.

"Oh, good," Marcy said. "So is Saturday afternoon okay for everybody?"

"There's a neat place across from the museum where we could get lunch," plump-cheeked Becky mentioned while they were nodding.

They agreed they'd be ready to go by eleven-thirty so that they could eat lunch together first. Wendy wrote down her address and telephone number for Sarah. "It's easy to find. The street's two blocks off State."

"Oh, I know where it is," Sarah said carelessly. She wadded up the slip of paper and stuck it in her pocket.

Wendy was hoping Sarah wouldn't lose her address when Becky leaned over and whispered something in Sarah's ear. Both the wadding and the whispering made Wendy very uncomfortable.

Don't start imagining bad things, she told herself as she pedaled her bike home through the streets of small one-family houses surrounding the school. This is your big chance. Marcy and her friends would start liking her once they saw how useful and agreeable she could be. Maybe they might start liking her enough to include her in their group permanently. She looked hopefully at the yellow school bus passing her on its way to the development of big, handsome homes where Marcy and Sarah lived, and smiled up at the bus windows in case one of them was looking out.

2

Waiting

Saturday morning Wendy woke up and wriggled her bare toes in the warmth of a sunbeam as she smiled to herself. Today was the museum trip with Marcy and Sarah's group. On Saturdays she usually lazed around in bed late, but she was too excited for dozing and daydreaming today. Was it early enough to catch Mother alone for a few minutes? Wendy needed some advice.

In Brooklyn, where Mother had worked in a department store as a fashion consultant sometimes six days a week, they'd specialized in cozy chats. Here in this midwestern city, even though Mother worked at home, Wendy practically had to make an appointment to see her. Either there were dressmaking customers, or Chick and Eric needed to be taken to Little League, or Mother was going out with Wally, or Ellen was demanding something from her. Ellen took up the most time. She'd started calling Mother "Mother" and pushing her claim to be the first kid in line as soon as Wally had announced they were getting married. But she hadn't used the word "sister" once.

The shower was running. Since nobody but Ellen let water run that long, it had to be her. Wendy listened for bangs and clatters to place Chick and Eric but heard only the jazz music that Mother liked to listen to as she worked.

"Time to go out and chase a butterfly," Wendy told her cat Tink. She got up with the black silk scarf of his warm body draped over her arm and almost stepped on a green snake wriggling an inch from her bare feet on the orange shag carpet.

Tink hissed and sailed out of her arms and under the dresser. Wendy peered at the snake with interest. She wasn't frightened by snakes or anything in nature. Leaning closer, she saw black threads attached to its body. Then she heard the slight shuffling outside her door. Fake! She stepped down hard on the plastic thing. Whichever of her stepbrothers was working it from the other side of the door jerked back, and the strings snapped.

"She broke it. Look she broke it off the strings!" That was Eric squeaking. Eric was only eight.

"We're going to get you," Chick menaced outside her door. His voice was deep for a nine year old's.

Wendy didn't say a word, but she tossed the plastic snake out the open window. If she'd known that having two little brothers meant being teased so much, she wouldn't have been eager for Mother to marry Wally. Having a big family had sounded like fun after being an only child for eleven years. Maybe it could be fun if the stepsister wasn't Ellen and the stepbrothers weren't Eric and Chick.

Tink rubbed against her ankles. Then he fixed his yellow eyes on her and showed his pink tongue as he merrowed an out-please request.

"Not now," she said. "It's enemy territory out there. Wait till the boys go away."

Silence from the hall. They could already have gone. The shower was still running. Mother said the reason Ellen spent so long in it was because she was getting used to her body. It seemed to Wendy that thirteen years was more than enough time for Ellen to have gotten used to her body. Wendy hadn't had hers as long, and it was so familiar that she found it boring. "Shall we peek and see if they're there?" Wendy asked her cat.

Tink rolled onto his side and arched his back so that his front and back paws met. His eyes squeezed shut in a yawn. He was a patient cat, more patient than Wendy. She tiptoed to the door and inched it open. The hall was empty except for the rag rug that ran past the four closed doors, three bedrooms and one bathroom. No doors were ever shut in Wendy and Mother's old Brooklyn apartment. But here, Wally had made shut bedroom doors the law because he got sick of all the complaints about violations of privacy upstairs. Part of the law was that any closed door had to be knocked on and nobody could go in anyone else's room without permission.

Wendy needed to use the toilet. She'd have to wait until Ellen left the bathroom. Having one bathroom for five people plus Ellen was the only fault Wendy found in this old-fashioned little house that Wally had inherited from his grandparents.

Tink scooted between Wendy's bare feet and ran downstairs.

"Gotcha," Eric squeaked from below. Tink yowled and Wendy rushed to the rescue.

Her stepbrothers were lying on top of pillows at the foot of the stairs. Wendy saw Tink squirm out from under the pillow pile and streak off through the living room.

"What're you doing to my cat? You could kill him shoving pillows on him like that . . . Mother!" Wendy called in frustration. She had no hope of making Chick and Eric behave. They'd listen to Ellen, but never to her.

Mother appeared in the doorway to the kitchen holding her pinking shears. "What's wrong?"

"They tried to suffocate my cat," Wendy complained.

"No, we didn't," Chick said. "We were playing bumper cars with pillows and we fell down."

"On top of the cat?" Mother asked. She narrowed her beautiful green eyes suspiciously at her stepsons, but her wide mouth twitched at the ends. The twitching meant Mother was trying not to laugh.

Wendy would have thought the boys were funny too if she weren't the one to find ice cubes in her bed on a cold winter night, or a cup of water spilling on her head when she opened a door, or her school books hidden when she was already late for school. They called her names too. Meg had advised her to be mean back. "You're too nice," Meg had claimed; "You let them get away with it." But meanness didn't come easily to Wendy.

"It was an accident," Chick told Mother, and he added in a smart aleck way, "Besides, the cat got away; so who cares?"

Instead of calling him on his tone, Mother just said earnestly, "Pets depend on us to treat them with tender loving care, Chick."

"Tink's not my pet," Chick said. "He's Wendy's."

"Just the same," Mother said, "you ought to be kind."

"I'm hungry," Eric said, distracting Mother from the subject of pet care.

"Didn't you boys eat breakfast?"

"You promised you'd make us pancakes," Eric said.

"So I did," Mother agreed. "I'll do it now." As usual she seemed relieved to forget and forgive them. "Want some, Wendy?"

"Sure," Wendy said. The bathroom door opened and closed upstairs. "Excuse me. I'll be right back," she said and took off.

She got back downstairs to find Eric and Chick finishing off their syrup-soaked pancakes and Mother on the phone with one of her dressmaking customers. There didn't seem to be any pancake batter left.

Wendy spread some peanut butter on crackers and asked the boys if they wanted to help her do the breakfast dishes.

Chick looked at her as if she were crazy. "That's a girl's job," he said, even though they both knew it wasn't. "Come on, Eric. Let's go."

They ran out the back door without asking Mother's permission, heading toward the big sandbox where they had all their construction trucks, piles of brick, and old two by fours. Unless they were up to something awful, Mother pretty much let them do what they wanted. "You've got to keep a firm hand on them," Wally kept telling her. Last week Wendy had heard Mother answer him that she hadn't had any practice disciplining kids because Wendy had been so good. It had made Wendy proud at the time. Now she was sorry she hadn't given Mother more practice. Wally's kids were wild.

"I've got to take Chick and Eric to their Little League game soon," Mother said when she finished her phone call. "And Ellen needs a costume for a dress rehearsal of the Memorial Day parade. Some other girl dropped out so Ellen's going to be lead majorette. She's pleased as punch about it."

"Good," Wendy said. "But what should I do about the museum trip with Marcy's group today, Mom? Do you think I should wear a skirt or pants?"

"Since when did *you* start worrying about clothes?" Mother asked in surprise. "Dont fret, Wendy, just relax and be yourself." Mother combed her slender fingers through the tangle of Wendy's sandy-colored curls. "My sunshine child," she said fondly and kissed Wendy.

If only the rest of the world found her as lovable as Mother did! "I don't care how I look," Wendy said, "but Sarah and Marcy are into clothes. Do you think my jeans skirt would be good?"

"Perfect," Mother said. She asked if Wendy had lunch money and went for her purse even though Wendy said she had enough money.

"Take this and have a super special something." Mother tried to tuck a bill in Wendy's pocket.

Wendy ducked away. "No, thanks, Mom." Mother was worrying about money now that she had to depend on Wally's earnings as a medical supplies salesman and what she could bring in from her dressmaking.

"I'll want to hear all about it later," Mother said.

"If you have time."

"I'm never too busy for you," Mother said and sighed. "I guess that's not true anymore, is it?" She didn't wait for Wendy's answer. "Well, Wally gets home tomorrow. It's easier when he's here."

"Whoops!" Wendy said noticing the time. "I've got to get dressed." She rushed upstairs and pulled on her jeans skirt and a clean top. She even tried to brush her hair which was hopeless because no matter what, it never looked neat. It would if she'd get it cut, Mother said, but Wendy enjoyed winding a curl around her finger and chewing on the end. She didn't like her wide mouth which was just like Mother's except on Wendy it didn't look as good. She didn't like her close-together eyes, either; but the jungly look of her hair, that she liked.

Back downstairs she watched for Sarah's mother's car through the plant-filled bay window behind the couch.

Mother called from the kitchen, "I'm leaving with the boys now. Have a good time, love." She blew a kiss.

"You too," Wendy said.

Tink's head poked between the leaves of a Boston fern and a peperomia plant. "Meow?" he asked.

"Yes, they're gone," she told him. "Want some breakfast?"

No doubt Sarah's mother would honk for her, Wendy thought, and she returned to the kitchen to feed Tink. With any luck Ellen would take her usual hour plus to get dressed, and Wendy would be long gone by the time she arrived downstairs. Tink sniffed disdainfully at the salmon for cats and licked his side instead of eating it. Feeling guilty about the waste, Wendy opened a can of chicken for cats and dumped the salmon. Chicken had been last week's favorite, but Tink had tired of it. Today it suited him. When he'd finished eating, she let him out.

By now it was past noon. It would be awful if Sarah's mother had gotten lost driving from her fancy suburb into the city to pick up Wendy. Of course, Becky and Jill rode a different bus from the one Marcy and Sarah took which meant they didn't live in The

Hills either. It might have taken longer to pick everybody up than Sarah's mother had expected.

Wendy thought about school buses. At first she had been glad she lived within walking distance of the school, just like in Brooklyn, but now she was sorry. A lot of socializing went on in the buses that she didn't get in on. Other than during lunch, kids didn't have time to just talk in school. That could be why she hadn't made friends except for Meg who'd also been a walker but had lived across town near the hospital. If the problem was just that kids hadn't gotten to know Wendy well enough yet, all she had to do was try to be more friendly. Or something.

The stairs squeaked. Wendy looked up and her jaw dropped at the sight of Ellen coming down.

"What are *you* staring at?" Ellen demanded.

"Is that your costume for the parade?" Wendy asked.

"Thanks a lot!" Ellen said indignantly. "You're always so nice to me when Mother's around. She should hear the way you make fun of me when she isn't."

"I'm not making fun of you," Wendy protested. Ellen looked a little like Wonderwoman today in blue and red silver foil. Her bleach-streaked hair was rolled into an enormous doughnut shape around her head. Red and blue eye makeup and red lipstick matched her clothing. Ellen wanted to be a rock star and already dressed like one.

"You're going out with those snobs from The Hills looking like that?" Ellen said.

Wendy looked down to check herself out. "What's

wrong?" She expected something was untucked, unbuttoned or untied as usual.

"Your hair's not even brushed," Ellen said, "and look at your shoes."

Now that Ellen drew her attention to them, Wendy saw that a strap had snapped across the toe. She wound a curl around her finger while she considered changing to her sneakers.

Ellen had come close now. She sniffed. "Yeech, peanut butter! Don't you care how fattening that stuff is?"

Wendy sucked her stomach in defensively. She wasn't fat, just a little fleshy compared to a carrot stick eating person like Ellen. "Umm," Wendy said. "I like peanut butter."

Ellen sniffed again in disgust and went clopping off to the kitchen in her backless shoes, probably for coffee. Mother had agreed to let her drink it so long as she filled half her cup with milk. Skim of course.

Dismayed by all the things Ellen had found wrong with her, Wendy chewed on her hair and tried to decide about the sneakers. The new ones made her big toes sore, and the old ones looked worse than the sandals. She couldn't trek through a museum if she wasn't comfortable. She got out Wally's stapler and tried to staple the broken strap in place, but it wouldn't stick.

Sarah's mother was half an hour late, then forty minutes late. Anxiously Wendy stared out the window, concentrating to make her come. She should have taken Sarah's telephone number, but she hadn't, and Brown was too common a name to look up without an address to go by.

Clip clop, Ellen was back. "You got stood up, didn't you?"

Wendy shrugged, too choked up to answer.

"Well, I'm not surprised," Ellen said. "So what are you going to do with yourself today?"

"I don't know. Leave me alone," Wendy mumbled.

"Well, you don't have to be so rude." Ellen clopped off in a huff.

It was hard to see with tears blurring her eyes, but Wendy kept her eyes on the street faithfully. She remembered Becky's whispering. But even if the others were capable of deliberately forgetting to pick her up, Marcy would never—would she? Wendy bit her lip. Something must be terribly wrong with her. They wouldn't be that mean for no reason. Tears slid down her cheeks in a shameful stream. "Don't be such a baby," she scolded herself, but the tears kept sliding, and finally she even sobbed a little. Luckily no one was around to notice.

At one-thirty, Wendy gave up. She only hoped Miss Pinelli wouldn't be annoyed that she hadn't gotten to the museum with the group. Monday she'd have to tell Miss Pinelli again that she wanted to work on her own—unless Marcy called meanwhile, unless Sarah's mother's car had broken down, unless they had meant to pick her up but somehow couldn't.

Honor at the Playground

Wendy retreated to her bedroom where everything was soft and comforting and her own. Curled up on the cushioned window seat beside the open window, she inhaled the new grass fragrance of the pearly spring day and tried to convince herself not to waste the rest of it. She saw Tink strolling toward the garden apartments that backed up to the yards of the small private homes on Wally's dead-end street. At night when people turned on lights in their apartments, Wendy could sometimes see silhouettes of people reading or cooking or eating. It gave her a sense of companionship in the dark.

A girl who looked like Honor was crossing between two clumps of brick apartments on the path to the playground. No doubt it was Honor because she lived in one of those apartments. The first time Wendy found that out, she'd invited Honor over after school, but Honor had said flatly, "No thanks. I don't have the time." It had surprised Wendy that anybody who looked as teddy bear plump and cuddly as Honor could be so cold. Honor's liquid brown eyes and ripe lips could still melt Wendy into a friendly puddle even though she'd learned that Honor didn't want anything to do with her.

Tink had disappeared from view. Honor was carrying a book. Going to the library maybe. She read a lot, mostly books by or about black people. It must feel strange to be the only black person in her class, Wendy thought, and wondered if that was why Honor kept to herself. The black girls in Brooklyn had hung around together, and making friends with them was hard. They didn't seem to like white kids. Would Honor like her if she were black? They'd had a good conversation at the end of school yesterday when Wendy had handed back the shared compositions for Miss Pinelli. Honor's had an A on it, of course. Honor got A's on everything. "You have such a beautiful handwriting," Wendy had said.

"Anybody can have a good handwriting if they take the time," Honor had answered.

"Not me. My pen kind of scrawls away from me even when I'm careful," Wendy had said.

A smile lit Honor's deep brown eyes. "Looks like you got an A anyway."

Then Wendy saw that the next paper was her own, and sure enough, a scarlet A stood out in the top margin. "I can't believe it!" Wendy had said. Usually she got a B+ or at best an A− because of punctuation and spelling errors.

"Miss Pinelli had tears in her eyes when she finished reading it," Honor had told her kindly.

That had been the longest and best conversation Wendy had had with Honor all year, even though they'd worked on the Christmas food committee together and sometimes been in the same group.

Wendy pulled back from the window. She couldn't stand being inside looking out another minute. With luck, she might find Mother free to go for a walk. By now, Ellen had surely left for her rehearsal, and the boys were still at their Little League game.

Opening the door to the enclosed porch which was Mother's workshop, Wendy put some cheer into her voice as she said, "Hi there again."

"Hi, darling," Mother said. "Ellen told me you weren't picked up. I thought you were asleep. As soon as I finish this costume for her, I'm going to go get the boys and take you to the museum."

"You don't have to take me to the museum," Wendy said, unwilling to pour her heart out in front of Ellen, who was leaning on the cutting table where Mother was snipping away at a bolt of vivid red material. "Anyway, I don't have the work sheets to fill out."

"I can't understand why they didn't at least call," Mother fretted.

"They probably just forgot me," Wendy said matter-of-factly.

"Oh, Wendy, they couldn't have." Mother gave her an anxious look. "Have you eaten lunch yet?"

"No, I'm not hungry."

"Don't make her eat," Ellen said. "She'd look a lot better if she took off a few pounds. Wouldn't she, Mother?"

"Wendy's not fat," Mother said.

"But you look better in clothes if you're on the thin side, right?" Ellen urged, as if Mother's agreement was important to her. "Isn't that why models are thin?"

"Wendy's not planning to be a model."

Wendy gauged the pile of work in progress that Mother had waiting for customers. It looked as if she was way behind, too behind to stop for a walk.

"What *are* you planning to be, Wendy?" Ellen asked in the concerned older sister voice she used when Mother was around. "A vet or something?"

"A nurse," Wendy said absently.

"A *nurse!* Nobody wants to be a nurse anymore."

"What'll happen to all the sick people in hospitals then?" Wendy asked.

"Wendy has a lot of empathy for people," Mother said. "She's a caring person."

"I guess you could say I'm sort of self-centered," Ellen said and slid a glance at Mother.

"Performing artists are supposed to be self-centered from what I've heard," Mother said neutrally.

The answer seemed to satisfy Ellen. She tossed her head, carefully so as not to disturb the doughnut hair, and said, "Well, I'm not a professional yet." Then she told Wendy, "This is a very special lady," meaning Mother.

"Your father's nice too," Wendy said politely.

"Dad's okay, but he doesn't understand how it is for a girl, not the way Mother does."

Mother began checking the fit of Ellen's costume on her. Wendy leaned her elbows on the cutting table. Mother's head was next to Ellen's, and it struck Wendy how alike they looked, both slim, dark haired, and graceful. All Wendy had of Mother was the wide mouth. Otherwise she was square, sandy colored, ordinary looking. Maybe Ellen was a more interesting daughter for a fashion consultant. The thought gave Wendy heartburn. She hated feeling jealous of Ellen, but lately she did sometimes. "Go ahead and hate her," Meg had said. "I would." A wave of missing Meg struck Wendy hard.

Rather than let it knock her down, Wendy said, "I think I'll go for a walk. See you guys later."

She followed Tinkerboy's path across the backyard, but instead of going under a bush she crossed the apartment house parking lot to the playground hidden behind the first clump of brick apartments. There was Honor sitting on a swing, rocking gently as she read.

She was the only one in the playground. No one was climbing on the railroad tie mountain. No one was on the slides or using the baby basket seat swings or the seesaw. Spring seemed to have cast a spell that had put everyone but Honor to sleep.

"Hi, Honor." Wendy took the slat swing next to hers.

Honor looked up, "Hi."

"Want a push?"

"No, thanks." Honor's eyes went back to her book.

Wendy persisted. "What are you reading?"

"Virginia Hamilton. She's a black writer." Honor showed Wendy the cover of the book with the title *Sweet Whispers, Brother Rush.* "It's good."

Wendy nodded. "Maybe I'll read it after you finish. Did you get it out of the school library?"

"No, the public one downtown. Their selection's better."

"I guess you'd rather read than anything, wouldn't you, Honor?"

"No, I'd rather eat than anything," Honor said promptly. "And you'd rather talk than anything. I know that." She turned her book around to resume reading. Wendy was hurt for an instant, but she remembered how kind Honor had been about her composition yesterday afternoon, so she put the hurt aside and tried again.

"The only time I ever got in trouble for talking was in music when Meg was leaving last month. I guess you weren't there."

Honor raised an eyebrow which made her look very superior, but she seemed to be listening. "See, it was Meg's last day, and I had things to tell her still," Wendy said. Unexpected tears filmed her eyes. Embarrassed, she wiped them away with the back of her hand and finished, "I thought it was mean of the music teacher to send me to the office just for talking."

"She probably didn't think about it being Meg's last day."

"Still," Wendy said. She looked at the railroad tie

mountain, surprised to find Tink perched on it watching her. "That's my cat. I didn't know he came this far."

"He's cute. I've seen him around before, or a black cat like him with white paws and a white chin."

"He likes to roam in nice weather, but he comes home at night to sleep with me. His name's Tink."

"Tink for Tinkerbell?" Honor asked, pushing against the ground to get more movement from the swing.

"Tinkerboy. He was Tinkerbell—you know from *Peter Pan* because I'm Wendy? But he turned out to be male."

"You're lucky to have a cat. I wish I could," Honor said.

"Why can't you?"

"No pets allowed in the apartments. Someone gave my grandma a rabbit for me last Christmas, but the building manager was fixing our toilet, and he saw it hopping around and told us to get rid of it. My grandmother even went to the owner. She was one of the first renters, so she has rights. But he wouldn't listen. He said rabbits are dirty and draw bugs—which is a lie. Grandma got so mad I was scared she'd have a heart attack."

"Do you live with just your grandmother?"

"Yes."

"Did your parents die?"

"My father did. Then my mother married someone else."

"Oh!" Wendy said in delight at finding something important in common with Honor. "My mother did too—marry someone else. And my father died, but I was so little I don't remember him."

"I remember my father very well," Honor said. She looked sad and soft.

"But how come you don't live with your mother?"

"You ask too many questions," Honor said.

"Sorry."

Honor glowered at her in sudden anger. "You just better never tell anyone."

"Tell anyone what?"

Honor groaned. "About me not living with my mother. Oh, I don't know why I bother telling you anything. Just forget it, hear?" She turned back to her book with determination.

"Well—" Wendy was confused. She fumbled for something to say that wouldn't offend Honor more. "Well, if you want to play with Tink any time, you're welcome to come to my house."

"No, thanks," Honor snapped.

"Why not?"

"Because he's your cat, not mine."

"Well, yes, but if you can't have one of your own —" Wendy was flustered so she babbled foolishly, "Like, I was friends with a lady's dog when we lived in Brooklyn. I visited him and played with him and she let me walk him sometimes."

"But the dog wasn't yours, so when you needed him, he wasn't there, right?"

"Yes, well, I see what you mean . . . it's like friends. Like a friend is someone you can call up when you need to talk, not just someone you bump in to and have a conversation with once in a while."

"Sort of," Honor agreed.

"Of course, someone you talk to once in a while could become a friend . . . like you and me," Wendy pointed out, but in her eagerness she pushed her swing, and since she was sitting on it crookedly, it banged into Honor's swing.

Honor popped off her seat and said fiercely, "We can't be friends."

"How come?"

"Because."

Finally Wendy accepted it. Honor just didn't like her. The dignified thing to do would be to get up and walk away and never speak to Honor again, but Wendy sat on in a crumpled heap. Honor's rejection right after Marcy's group's not showing up that morning was just too much.

"What's the matter with you?" Honor said.

Wendy didn't answer and Honor fidgeted. Then she offered, "I could lend you this book after I finish it tonight. It's got two weeks left on it before it has to go back."

"That's okay. I can get it out on my own card."

"Okay," Honor said and began walking away. As she passed the railroad tie mountain where Tink was still sitting, she reached out a finger to stroke Tink's head.

"Honor, you ready to go?" A bulky looking, older woman in a gray suit and hat that matched her gray hair stood on the walk. Her skin was browner than Honor's, but she held herself in the same proud, solid way, and looked at Wendy as fiercely as Honor had when she was angry.

"I'm ready, Grandma," Honor said.

"Who's that you were talking to?" the grandmother asked.

"Nobody," Honor said and left without looking back at Wendy.

Nobody, Wendy thought and shivered. Sadly she picked Tink up and headed home. As she was crossing her own backyard, she saw Ellen in the hammock under the trees near the back door.

"Tink run away?" Ellen looked up from her magazine to ask.

"No. He was just visiting the playground."

"My friend has a pair of Siamese cats, but one of them bites. Tinker's pretty nice that way, isn't he?"

Wendy approached Ellen warily. "I didn't know you liked cats."

"I don't, usually. But Tinker's come into my room a couple of times. He likes the glass chimes on my window." Ellen ran one of her long red nails down Tink's back as Wendy held him. Tink stretched sensuously.

Wendy leaned on one hip, prepared to be sociable as long as Ellen was. "Do you want to hold him?"

"See if he'll stay in the hammock with me," Ellen

said. She took Tink and set him down beside her, but as soon as she released him, he sprang out of the hammock and disappeared around the house.

"I guess he's not much for hammocks," Wendy said. "Did you get back from your rehearsal already?"

"My teacher called and made it for five o'clock. She had an emergency."

Wendy looked toward the house, and Ellen must have read her mind because she said, "Mother's gone to pick up the boys from the Little League game. She told me to tell you she'll be back soon."

"I guess I'll have a snack then," Wendy said.

"Rock the hammock for me first?"

"Sure." Ellen's friendly moods didn't come often or last long, and Wendy had long since decided that she didn't like Ellen all that much. Still, she was willing to meet niceness with niceness. She pushed the hammock gently.

"Harder," Ellen ordered. "See if you can knock me out of it."

"What for?"

"For fun."

Wendy pushed harder. "Don't you get dizzy?" she asked.

"Never," Ellen boasted. She closed her eyes, pretending to fall asleep.

Why was she such a show-off? Wendy thought. Finally, she said, "I'm going now. I'm hungry." She gave Ellen one last mighty push and walked away. Ellen rolled out of the hammock onto her hands and knees. "Oh, I'm sorry!" Wendy said.

"You idiot. You could've killed me." Ellen stood up and looked at her red silver foil pants which sure enough were split up the back. "Look what you did to my new outfit!"

"You told me to do it hard," Wendy defended herself. Ellen ran into the house with her hand gripping the seams of her pants. Wendy grinned at the sight, which was a bad mistake, because at the back door Ellen turned to say something to her and saw the grin.

"You'll be sorry, you sneak," Ellen said. "I'm telling Mother what you did to me."

Wendy stayed in the kitchen, eating a cream cheese and raisin sandwich very slowly because she wanted to be the first to talk to Mother as soon as she walked in. A car horn honked and Ellen ran downstairs and out the front door. Someone was probably picking her up to go to her rehearsal. Wendy relaxed. Now she'd be able to explain to Mother what had happened before Ellen got in her version of the story. A few minutes later, Mother came through the living room into the kitchen looking upset.

"What did you do to Ellen, Wendy?"

"Nothing."

"She just told me you knocked her out of the hammock deliberately. She was practically in tears."

"Ellen asked me to swing her. She kept making me do it harder and harder."

Mother frowned. "Why would she do that?"

"I don't know. To show how great she is. I hate her."

"Oh, Wendy, don't say such a thing, please." Mother set down her bag of groceries but she still looked burdened.

Just then the back door flew open and Chick asked, "Mom, could you talk to the lady next door? She's got our ball and won't give it back."

"Were you throwing that ball near Mrs. Vail's flower bed again, Chick?" Mother followed him out to the yard as he forcefully presented his side of the action. Wendy considered unloading the bag of groceries, but she couldn't get up the energy. She felt low, under the basement stairs low. Wearily, she climbed up to her room and shut herself in.

It was extraordinary how many things could go wrong on such a beautiful spring day. She'd been stood up by Marcy's group, snubbed by Honor, and treacherous Ellen had gotten her in trouble with Mother. Today had to be some kind of record all-time low in her life. About the only good thing Wendy could think of was that tomorrow had to be better.

4

Baby-sitting

Wally returned home early from his sales trip. He walked in Saturday evening and bellowed, "Surprise!" and they all rushed into the kitchen to greet him. In the midst of the excitement, with everyone talking at once, Wally said he was taking them out for dinner. Mother said she couldn't go. She had another couple of hours of work on a suit an oversized lady needed for a wedding the next day. "What are you working yourself to death for?" Wally demanded. "Let your fat lady wear something else."

"She can't fit into last year's dress, Wally. I promised her."

"All right, we'll wait for you," he said. "Meanwhile, I can catch up with the kids' lives."

Wendy was impressed that his children immediately settled into chairs around the kitchen table without complaint. "So what's new?" he asked, getting himself a beer from the refrigerator. Wally was pudgy and snub-nosed with only a fringe of hair left, and he reminded Wendy of Humpty Dumpty, but he was a beautiful listener.

Ellen went first. She told about how she'd become lead majorette in the Memorial Day parade. "You better be in town for that, Daddy, or I'll be mad at you."

"You can count on it, babe. I love parades almost as much as I love you."

Chick described the afternoon's Little League game with some help from Eric, and Wally said he was sorry he'd missed it. "How about you, Wendy? What've you got to say for yourself?"

"Nothing," Wendy said.

"You don't sound too happy, toots. Still missing your friend?"

"Wendy keeps writing her letters and hasn't gotten any back," Ellen said.

"Well, Thailand is a long ways off," Wally said, "and it'll probably take a while to get settled in. Her parents are working in a hospital there, right?" Wally asked.

"Right," Wendy said and explained, "Meg's not much for writing letters. She already told me that."

"So find a new friend," Wally said. "You're an outgoing kid. You shouldn't have any problem."

"Personally, I think having several friends is better," Ellen said. "The best friend stuff is childish anyway."

Wendy stared at her stepsister. What was Ellen talking about? All Ellen had were acquaintances who appeared and disappeared like stage props in her life. Now that she wanted to be a rock star, the girls she called were in her voice and dance classes. She talked behind their backs and traded on their secrets. If she liked a boy, she'd be friends with his sister or his friends' girlfriends. All she did was use people. To Wendy, being a friend meant being loyal.

"Mrs. Vail stole our baseball and Mom got it back, but now we can't practice in our backyard," Eric put in. "Mom told Mrs. Vail we wouldn't."

"You're lucky you got your ball back," Wally pointed out and added, "I guess you're old enough now to practice in the street if you're careful about cars." Their dead-end street only had six houses.

Later they went to Wally's favorite Italian restaurant and everybody ordered the special, which was lasagna, except for Ellen who had eggplant parmigiana. Wally told them about his sales trip and how he had seen a deer with fawns grazing right beside the highway one evening. Then he talked about an old customer of his who was dying of cancer but still making jokes. "He lives at the far end of nowheresville, but I never minded the drive because I looked forward to talking to him. I'm going to miss that guy."

On their way home, Wally asked, "Any young women in the car want to volunteer to keep tabs on the boys tomorrow afternoon? Your mother and I have some shopping to do and a housewarming to go to at four."

"We don't need baby-sitters," Chick protested.

"Did I say baby-sitters?" Wally asked. "You guys can get pretty wild, and I just want to be sure the house is still standing when I get home . . . how about it, girls?"

"I can't," Ellen said quickly. "I'm doing a school project at a friend's tomorrow afternoon."

"Wendy?"

She slipped back from her daydream about how a new girl would be in her class on Monday, and how Wendy would tell Marcy that since they'd forgotten to pick her up and the new girl needed a partner, Wendy was going to team up with her. "Watch the boys? I don't think I can," Wendy said in alarm.

"Wendy!" Mother sounded hurt. "You know how little time Wally and I have alone. Couldn't you manage to take care of your brothers *one* afternoon?"

"Well, but—if they'll listen to me."

"Sure they will," Wally assured her. "They'll hear from me when I get back if they don't."

Wendy doubted the threat was powerful enough, judging by Chick's devilish look and Eric's frown, but she didn't protest further.

*

Sunday Wendy slept until nearly noon. By the time she got downstairs, Wally and Mother were dressed up and ready to leave.

Ellen fingered Mother's linen and cotton shift which was woven in interesting designs. "You look so stunning. I bet nobody even *sees* anybody else at that housewarming," Ellen said.

"What about me?" Wally asked, poking out his chest. "Don't I look stunning too?"

Ellen wrinkled her nose disapprovingly. "You look like final sale markdowns, Dad."

"How could you tell?" He looked so comical holding his arm out to peer at his denim jacket in pretended amazement that everybody laughed. It had been Wally's lack of clothes sense that brought Mother and him together. He'd hailed her as she was passing through the men's department to ask her opinion on a shirt and tie combination because, as Mother had told Wendy afterward, he had said Mother looked like a woman with classy taste.

A horn tooted, and Ellen called good-bye and ran out with the box of materials for the diorama she and another girl were supposed to build.

"We'll bring back a giant chocolate chip cookie for every good kid in the family," Mother promised.

"What about good adults?" Wally said.

"Good adults don't eat chocolate chip cookies the size of saucers unless they want to get fat," Mother said and delicately poked Wally's paunch.

"Wendy," Wally appealed. "Do you think I'm fat?"

"I'll share my chocolate chip cookie with you," Wendy said. "I shouldn't eat a whole one either."

Wally groaned. "Honest women. Why did I marry into a family of honest women?" As he and Mother left, he said to Wendy, "You won't have any trouble with them, ducky. I gave them strict instructions to behave." He hugged her and knuckled her cheek gently, saying, "You're the prize in my Cracker Jack box, you know that?"

At that moment she would have taken charge of a roomful of monsters for him.

"Have a good afternoon, kids," Mother said, and when she kissed Wendy good-bye, she whispered, "Luck."

"Dad sure talks silly sometimes," Chick said when he and Eric and Wendy were alone.

Looking at the fine rain sifting by the windows, Wendy said, "It's a good day for playing Monopoly, isn't it?"

"Yeah, okay," Chick said. "I'll get the set."

The game began well. Wendy made herself a peanut butter sandwich and ate it while she played. In between turns, she went back in the kitchen and mixed up three banana milkshakes which she served with straws in tall glasses. Meanwhile she reminded herself that she didn't have to make Chick and Eric go to bed or take baths or do anything they didn't like. All she had to do was keep them from hurting themselves and/or wrecking the house.

"I passed Go." Eric held his hand out for his two hundred dollars to Wendy, who was banker.

"I wish it would stop raining," Chick said. "Let's go out anyway and pretend it's not."

"I'd rather play Monopoly," Eric said. He'd bought up some of the best property, and now he asked, "Can I buy a hotel?"

"Not till you get three houses on each property,

dummy," Chick told him. "Besides, you don't have enough money. He doesn't have enough money, does he, Wendy?"

"He will if one of us lands on him," Wendy said.

Chick's move was to Free Parking and Eric completed his set of houses on all three orange properties which made his rents expensive. It was Wendy's turn to roll the dice. She made it safely past Eric. Chick didn't. He landed smack on the highest rent property Eric had.

Eric screeched with joy and told his brother, "You owe me a lot. Boy, do you owe me a lot. Doesn't he, Wendy?" Eric showed her his card.

Wendy told Chick how much he owed.

"And now I can buy a hotel, right?" Eric was so excited he bounced off his seat.

"It's not your turn, and you're not going to buy anything because I'm not playing any more," Chick said furiously. A sweep of his arm knocked everything off the board.

"Chick, what's wrong with you? It's just a game," Wendy said. "Last time we played, you won. Besides, just because Eric's ahead doesn't mean—"

"I don't care. This is a boring game. Let's go outside and jump in puddles. That'd be *fun*."

"We could play a different game," Wendy offered. "Or how about getting out your race car set?" She didn't care what they played as long as it was inside where she could most easily control them.

Eric peered between Mother's spider plant and

ferns. "Hey, it stopped raining. It really did, Wendy. Let's go to the playground."

They looked so eager and the sun was poking inviting fingers through holes in the cloud cover. It shouldn't be that hard to watch them in the playground. "Okay," Wendy agreed.

They bounded to the door. She thought of puppies and wished she could leash them. "Hey, you have to wear jackets. It's pretty cool out."

"No, it's not. It's spring."

"If you don't put on your jackets, you can't go."

"Who says?" Chick's frown challenged her. "We can do what we want. Can't we, Eric?"

"Dad said we had to listen to her," Eric said uncertainly.

"But she can't tell us what to wear. She's not our mother. Come on, Eric. We don't need jackets."

They were out the door before Wendy could decide her next move. She grabbed her windbreaker from the hall closet and ran after them, pulling it on as she went. Chick charged straight through the biggest puddle in the parking lot. Wings of water sprayed out from his feet. Eric stopped, crouched, and sprang smack into the middle of the puddle.

"Did you see me splash, Chick?" he yelled gleefully.

They were already climbing wrong way up the wet slide when Wendy arrived. "Don't do that!" she yelled in a panic as Chick lay belly down at the top of the slide with his chin hooked over the edge. "Turn around, Chick. You'll hurt yourself."

Eric was the one who did. Halfway up the slide, he began to slip backward. He slid standing all the way down and toppled off.

"Are you all right?" Wendy ran to kneel beside him on the wet ground. He didn't look too sure of his own condition. She pulled him to a sitting position and saw that his back was coated with mud.

"Let go," he said, deciding to be brave. "I'm okay." He felt his arm. "Last time I broke my arm and had to get a cast. All the kids in my class signed it."

"Do you think you broke your arm again?" Wendy had no idea what to do if he had. Get him to the hospital probably, but how?

"He's okay," Chick said. "He's just scared."

"I am not."

"Well, then, come on. Let's slide down double."

"Now listen," Wendy said firmly. "We're going home if you can't play nice."

"Come on, Wendy. You come up too, and we can slide down triple."

"No thanks. I'll just watch."

This time they went up the ladder. Then, with Eric in front and Chick grasping him around the middle, they slid down together. Expecting disaster any minute, Wendy leaned against one of the poles that braced the swings' framework and watched. From a distance, Chick and Eric looked like such cute kids, but they were as full of mischief as the little brother Marcy had described in her composition. Wendy imagined calling to ask Marcy for tips on the handling of little brothers. "By the way," Wendy could say after they'd chatted a while, "what happened yesterday? You were supposed to pick me up, remember?" Then Marcy would make some excuse. If it was a really good excuse, being stood up wouldn't hurt so much. Wendy sighed, admitting to herself that she'd never call. She was too ashamed of being the kind of person anyone would treat so badly.

Two big boys and a kindergarten-sized girl were climbing on the railroad tie mountain. Chick and Eric left the slide and ran to join them. "Look at me!" the agile little girl yelled from the topmost peak. She stood there with her arms out, balancing precariously. Wendy couldn't believe it when she saw Chick grab the girl's ankle.

"Chick, you leave her alone. You'll make her fall."

A boy bigger then Wendy did something more effective than yelling. He pulled Chick's pants down. Chick squawked and let go of the girl's ankle to grab for his pants. He teetered, hauling up his pants, while Wendy screamed. The big boy and a stumpy kid with him were both laughing.

Pants in place again, Chick scrambled from the mountain. His next feat was to stand up on one of the board swings. A few knee bends and he was swinging up practically parallel to the ground. Wendy held her breath. She knew better than to try to stop him now, when he had been publicly humiliated. Eric, of course, got on the swing next to his brother and began imitating him.

"Bratty kids, aren't they?" Honor said. Wendy hadn't seen her approaching.

"They're my stepbrothers."

"Are you watching them or something?"

"I'm supposed to be."

"Lucky you," Honor said.

"I think they've just got spring fever," Wendy said.

"Is that why they're trying to break their necks?"

Wendy chewed at a stretch of lower lip, thinking hard. "I could suggest we make cookies. They like making cookies."

"Who doesn't?"

"Do you, Honor? I mean, would you want to?"

Honor considered. "I guess so. What kind we going to make?"

Wendy's heart gave a high kick at Honor's sudden friendliness, but she hid her surprise and said, "Plain sugar. That's all I know the recipe for."

"Better make your move now," Honor said. "Here come the troublemakers." She rolled her eyes toward the two bigger boys who appeared to be stalking the swinging Eric and Chick like prey.

"Hey, you guys, I'm going home to make cookies. Want to come help?" Wendy yelled.

Chick looked down behind him, saw the bigger boys, and promptly slid to the seat and jumped off at a run. "Yeah," he said.

Wendy saw the biggest boy wrap his arms around Eric's knees and pull. "Get away, you bum!" Eric cried.

"You let my brother go!" Wendy yelled and charged the swing set. The stumpy kid laughed at her. He put his fists up as if she were challenging him to fight, and threw a mock punch at her.

She stepped back and told the big one, "What are you being such a bully for? My brother didn't do anything to you."

"He's using my swing," the big one said. "I don't like kids using my swing. You live in this project?"

"No, we don't."

"Well, where do you live?"

"None of your business."

"Yeah, well you better get going before I get mad."

"Let go of my brother and we'll all get going," Wendy said.

"I'm keeping him for a hostage."

"I'll get the building superintendent," Honor said, and she started off with Chick at her heels.

"Let him go," the stumpy kid whispered to the tall one.

"I'm not afraid of the super. What's he going to do to me? Yell?"

"Come on," his buddy said. "You wanna get in trouble again?"

Suddenly the big one picked Eric up by the armpits and held him high over his head. "Want to get down, kid? Say please, pretty please, with sugar on it."

Wendy's fingers tightened into fists. She itched to punch the bully, or kick him in the shins, but she knew she wasn't strong enough to force him to release Eric. "Say it, Eric. Tell him 'please.' Please!"

Eric folded his lips firmly into his mouth and stared down at his tormentor who shook him a little, as if to shake the words out of him.

"Please, please let him go," Wendy begged.

Then Eric tried to kick the big kid who roared, "Hold his legs, Everett. Pull his sneakers off."

Eric struggled, and Wendy leaped into action and yanked at the big kid's arm. He let go of Eric, who fell down. Everett got Eric's sneakers, and the two big boys ran away with them. "Those are my new sneakers!" Eric cried.

Honor came charging back. "I couldn't find the super. Sunday's his day off, I think. How'd you get rid of them?"

"Me and Wendy beat them up," Eric said proudly.

"Where's your sneakers?" Chick asked as he pulled up next to Honor.

"They took them."

"Boy, Dad's going to be mad at you," Chick told Eric happily.

"Are we going to make cookies now?" Eric asked Wendy.

"Sure," Wendy said. She thought Eric had been pretty brave. "Want Honor and me to each take an arm and swing you across the parking lot?"

"No, thanks," Eric said. "I swung enough today."

Honor laughed.

The boys led the way home with Eric running through the wet grass in his socks. They got there to find Wendy had left the back door open.

"Some baby-sitter you are," Chick mocked.

"Listen, kid, she won't tell about all the bad things you did if you don't tattle on her," Honor said. "Right, Wendy?"

"I don't care," Wendy said. "I don't mind explaining why I ran out of the house in such a hurry that I left the door open."

"I won't tell," Chick said quickly. "If you won't."

Once inside, Chick said he and Eric could play their spaceman game while Wendy and Honor made the cookies. "I wanna help with the cookies," Eric said. Chick looked startled. It was the first time Wendy could remember Eric ever having gone against his brother's wishes.

"You can roll out the dough, Eric," she said to encourage him.

"Or sprinkle sugar on the pieces I cut," Honor said.

"We could make funny faces on the cookies," Chick said.

Nobody commented on his decision to join them. Wendy just said, "That's a good idea. I think there's raisins, and some walnuts we could chop up."

As a cooperative effort, the cookie baking was a big success, although few cookies made it into the oven because most of the dough was eaten raw.

"I love raw dough," Eric said.

"Me too," Honor agreed.

"Are you Wendy's friend?" Eric asked.

"No, just an acquaintance."

"What's the difference?" Chick asked Wendy.

"I don't know," Wendy said.

"Sure you do," Honor said. "You're the one with the scoop on friendship."

"What do you mean?"

"That composition you wrote about friendship. Remember? The one Miss Pinelli gave you an A on about you and Meg and how you were just alike. You said you both had the same color hair and had birthdays in May and liked talking on the phone every night. And you always knew if you watched a TV program she'd be watching the same one because you like the same things."

Wendy stared wide-eyed at Honor. Why had those details stuck in Honor's head? Or was Honor so smart she couldn't help remembering everything?

"Are we going to see how these cookies taste baked?" Honor asked.

"Sure. Let's have some with milk. Or would you rather have soda?" Wendy asked, remembering she was the hostess.

"Soda," Eric and Chick said at the same time.

"What I'd like's a cup of tea," Honor said. "I always have tea with my grandmother this time of day, but I'll drink milk if you have it."

"Do you have any brothers?" Eric asked.

"I have stepbrothers like you, but they don't count because they're white," Honor said.

"Why don't they count? I don't get it," Eric said.

"They don't count as relatives is what I mean," Honor said. "Because we're different colors."

"That's weird," Chick said.

"No, it isn't," Honor said. She looked at Wendy. "Is it?"

Wendy was still stuck in midsurprise from hearing that Honor had white stepbrothers. Had her mother married a white man then, or what? Honor was more interesting than a mystery book. If only she'd stay around long enough for Wendy to get to the last page! "I think inside differences count lots more than skin color," Wendy said finally.

"Being black makes you different inside," Honor said.

"How?" Wendy asked.

Honor considered. "I don't know exactly."

Wendy was thoughtful as she poured. She was beginning to understand why Honor wouldn't be her friend. It wasn't that Honor didn't like her, but that Wendy was white. She wondered if it was Honor's stepfather who'd made her hate white people.

After Honor left, Eric said, "Anyway, that girl's not black. She's more like permanently suntanned. Do you like her, Wendy?"

"I like her a lot," Wendy said. But there was nothing she could do about it. Neither she nor Honor could change the color of their skins.

*

None of them could eat the big chocolate chip cookies Mother and Wally had bought at the mall. Wendy suggested they save them for after-school snacks and everyone agreed that was a good idea.

"So how did the baby-sitting go?" Wally asked.

"Fine." Wendy smiled at Chick.

He looked away but Eric said, "We had a good time."

"I'm afraid Eric's going to need new sneakers," Wendy said.

"He just got a pair last week," Wally protested.

"We went to the playground—because it was so nice out—and a big kid stole them," Wendy explained. "I don't know who he was."

"What a shame," Mother said. "Can you fit into your old sneaks until I get to the store to buy another pair, Eric?"

"Sure," Eric said. And to Wendy's relief, that was that.

Before she went to sleep, she wrote Meg all about it, about the boys being rowdy and how Honor had suddenly decided to join them. "Even if she wanted to be friends, it would be hard," Wendy wrote, "because I don't understand her. One time she's nice and the next time she's not. You were always the same, Meg, and I miss you."

New Kid

Monday morning in homeroom, Marcy rushed over to Wendy's desk and said breathlessly, "Wendy, about the museum, I bet you thought we forgot you Saturday, but we didn't. What happened was Sarah's mother couldn't take us, and so at the last minute we had to get hold of everybody about when else they could go, and I kept trying your number but nobody answered or else your phone was busy. Maybe you ought to ask Miss Pinelli if you can work with some group that didn't start yet."

"But if you haven't gone to the museum yet—" Wendy said.

"We went Sunday."

"Oh," Wendy said.

"Most of the work is done, really," Marcy said, "and I know you wouldn't feel right getting credit when you didn't do anything. Really, you'll be better off in another group."

Wendy flushed and let Marcy walk away without another word.

"Believe that and she'll tell you another one," Honor said. Sitting next to Wendy, she'd overheard the conversation.

"She never called," Wendy said. "I was there waiting and nobody called."

"That girl's the worst gold-plated phony!"

Honor's indignation gave Wendy the courage to ask hopefully, "Would you let me into your group, Honor?"

"Okay with me, but ask Barbara," Honor said. "She's the leader."

Warily, Wendy approached Barbara in the hall on the way to gym.

"Oh, no, our group's too big already," Barbara protested. "I hate big groups. Nobody takes responsibility and I end up doing all the work."

There was no way around it; Wendy had to work alone. She explained it to Miss Pinelli quickly while the class was spinning off to the cafeteria for lunch. Miss Pinelli raised an eyebrow and said, "Let me think about that."

By the time Wendy got to the cafeteria, the only seat left was at the end of a table full of boys. She sat down and ate her lunch quietly. They ignored her, even moving away from her as if she had something catching. She couldn't hide in a book because she'd forgotten to bring one; so she started another letter to Meg, and eventually the half-hour lunch period ended.

Math came after lunch. Wendy concentrated on the practice problems on her work sheet. The room was so quiet she could hear paper sighing on desk tops and the scratching of pencils. Miss Pinelli liked quiet. She said it was the sound of real work. No wonder Miss Pinelli hated Jeremy. Already he was beginning to wriggle as if his outsized clothes bothered him. His chair squeaked on the tile floor. "Gotcha!" he called out. Miss Pinelli narrowed her eyes at him, and his voice sank to a mumble low enough for her to ignore, but Wendy could hear him. He'd moved into Meg's old seat next to hers.

"Grrr," Jeremy growled. The menacing sound was funny coming from pale, innocent-looking Jeremy. He was busy drawing monster pictures on his work sheet instead of answering the questions. What would Miss Pinelli do to him when she found out? He'd already lost his recesses for the rest of the term. She'd threatened to keep him back if he didn't complete his work, and she was strict enough to do it.

Wendy didn't like seeing Jeremy in trouble. Kids had nicknamed him Germy and didn't have much to do with him because he was a little goofy, but he was a good-natured boy. To nudge him into action, Wendy sent him a note. "Germy, the first answer is 'right angle.'"

Jeremy looked at her note and turned around. His voice rang out in the quiet room as he said, "Thanks, Wendy."

"What are you thanking Wendy for, Jeremy?" Miss Pinelli demanded.

Wendy held her breath, certain she was in for trouble. Jeremy jumped to his feet, took a step, and promptly tripped on his laces which were out of all but the last eyes of his high-topped sneakers. "She told me my shoelaces are untied, Miss Pinelli," Jeremy said.

Snickers rippled through the classroom before a glance from Miss Pinelli sent them all back to work. Jeremy's sneakers were always untied. He could be expected to trip over them at least once a day. Wendy tore off a corner of her work sheet and in tiny letters wrote, "Thanks." She waited a while before slipping it onto Jeremy's desk.

Honor was reading a book on Africa. She'd been the first to finish the work sheet. Sarah and Marcy were exchanging papers with Becky and Jill, checking to see that they all got the same answers. Last month they all four got the same answers wrong on a test, and Miss Pinelli had made them stay after class and write an explanation of how that had happened. Then she'd called their parents about it, and now all four girls said they hated Miss Pinelli. They'd even gotten up a petition to tell the principal that Miss Pinelli was too strict and tried to get everyone in the class to sign it.

Honor and Wendy and Meg wouldn't. Then Jeremy had crossed his name off the list, and Hee Chung and Dorothy said they wouldn't sign unless everybody else did. Marcy and Sarah had dropped the petition. Wendy wondered if they could still be holding a grudge against her for not signing, and if that was why they hadn't let her join their group.

The other Sarah, Sarah P., went up to take a tissue from the box on Miss Pinelli's desk. The other Sarah was sniffling as usual. She asked Miss Pinelli to shut the window near her desk. "It's warm out," the boy behind the other Sarah complained. "We'll all suffocate."

"Well, I can't help it," Sarah P. whined. "The air bothers my allergies."

"Can't she sit somewhere else?" the boy asked.

"Possibly, but meanwhile, we'll close the window," Miss Pinelli said, and that was that.

Hee Chung and Dorothy got up and tiptoed off to their violin lessons. They were both small slender girls, but Hee Chung had a face like a velvet-petaled pansy while Dorothy's face was sharp and narrow. Wendy had once invited Hee Chung to her house, but Hee Chung had nothing to say. Talking to her was as impossible as playing hide and seek solo. Suddenly Jeremy stood up.

"What are you getting up for, Jeremy?" Miss P. asked.

"I'm done."

"Stay seated and I'll come check your paper."

"Can't I just go look out the window till you're ready?"

"No."

Jeremy sat, but he slithered under his desk so that only his head remained visible above it. When Jeremy got restless he could make a pretzel look straight, and he was always restless.

Today he was lucky. Miss Pinelli asked for the work sheets to be passed down the rows and didn't look at Jeremy's.

Time for English. Wendy stiffened. If she was going to be an outcast, she hoped Miss Pinelli would let her work in the library so that nobody would see her working all by herself. But Miss Pinelli was busy talking to Barbara's group. Oh, please don't *force* me on Barbara, Wendy prayed. That would add humiliation to humiliation, and Wendy would choke if she had to swallow anymore. Miss Pinelli finished talking to Barbara's group and turned around.

"Get up off the floor, Jeremy," Miss Pinelli said. "Who are you supposed to be working with?"

"Nobody."

"You prefer to work alone?"

"No, but nobody prefers to work with me. I could work with you, couldn't I, Miss Pinelli?" His enthusiasm for the idea made him pop to his feet like a jack-in-the-box. "I could be the gofer and get all the books kids need from the library and stuff like that. Right? Isn't that a great idea?" He took two excited steps as if to start for the library right away.

"Stop!" Miss Pinelli held her hand up like a traffic cop and Jeremy halted with one foot in the air, long shoelaces dangling. That got another laugh from the class. He grinned as if he'd accomplished something.

"Wendy and Honor and Sarah P. will be forming a new group," Miss Pinelli said to him. "You can work with them."

"If you're sticking them with the other Sarah, it's

not fair to make them take me too," Jeremy protested on their behalf.

"That's okay, Jeremy," Honor said. "You can be our idea man."

Wendy didn't say anything. She was delighted to find herself in a group after all.

"What's an idea man?" Jeremy asked.

"Jeremy, stop talking and get to work . . . please," Miss Pinelli added. "Now whose group needs some direction?" Bruce raised his hand and Miss Pinelli approached him and Jason.

Under Honor's direction, the new group bumped their desks together. It was Jeremy who asked the question uppermost in Wendy's mind. "How come you got out of Barbara's group, Honor?"

"She's too bossy," Honor said. "Two bossy people in one group's bad."

"Who's the other bossy person?" Jeremy asked.

"Me," Honor said. "Now sit down and pay attention."

The other Sarah arrived, dragging a chair behind her, and sneezed wetly all over Honor's desk. "Why'd you decide not to work by yourself?" Honor asked her with a disgusted look.

"Miss Pinelli wouldn't let me," the other Sarah said. "She says working in groups is good for your social development or some dumb thing."

Honor grimaced. "Do you have any tissues?"

"I'll get them," Jeremy offered and scooted off. Once he'd told Wendy that the worst part of school was having to sit still, and next worst was teachers who yelled at him. "It hurts my ears," he'd said. Most of Jeremy's teachers ended up yelling at him.

They elected Honor the leader. Then they decided to write their report from filmstrips. Miss Pinelli had a box of them ready on the resource table in front of the room. "We might as well start," Honor said. "You want to get the projector and the filmstrips, Wendy?"

"Sure," Wendy said happily. She hoped Honor wouldn't get too discouraged working with her and Jeremy and Sarah P. The work would have been easier for her if she'd stayed with Barbara's group, but Honor seemed pretty calm about it. Well, Honor was capable of handling just about anything, Wendy imagined.

"I like filmstrips when they run backwards," Jeremy said. He put the whole box of tissues in front of Sarah P. "They're more fun that way."

"Germy, we'll need your help picking out the important points to write down, okay?" Honor said. "Who wants to be secretary?"

"Nobody can read my handwriting, but I'll do it if you want," Wendy said.

"How about you writing things down," Honor suggested to the other Sarah.

"My hand gets tired when I write too much."

"I'll write. I'll do it," Jeremy said.

"No, thanks," Honor said quickly. Nobody could read Jeremy's slapdash scribble, not even Jeremy. "I'll do it myself."

"That's not fair," Wendy said. "You'll end up doing all the work."

"Well, that's better than wasting time arguing," Honor said crossly.

"Why?" Jeremy asked. "She'll just give us more work as soon as we finish this. They always got more work for you to do."

Honor stared at him. Then she grinned and said, "Germy, you *do* make a lot of sense in your own fool way."

"Let's take turns reading aloud," the other Sarah said. Reading aloud was one thing she liked.

Jeremy looked over his shoulder to see what was going on in the rest of the class. Wendy nudged his elbow. "You start, Jeremy," she said.

After school that day, Wendy was unlocking her bike from the bike rack when she saw Honor walking away down the sidewalk. "Honor," Wendy called, "are you going to the playground this afternoon?"

Honor frowned at her and said brusquely, "No, I'm busy this afternoon."

Wendy got the message fast this time. She wasn't to assume they'd become friends just because they'd spent part of a weekend together and were working in the same group. But how could Wendy have guessed that after Honor had been so nice? Maybe Honor was too complicated for Wendy ever to figure her out.

*

There was no problem of who to sit with at lunch the next day. On Tuesdays an extra class was jammed into the cafeteria, and they all had to sit squeezed shoulder to shoulder across from each other at two long tables. Nobody could feel left out.

The smell of garlic in the meat sandwich of the boy on her left made Wendy slightly nauseous. She turned toward the other Sarah who was sitting on her right, complaining that her mother had given her peach yogurt instead of boysenberry. Across the table Jeremy was scrounging from the rejected parts of other kids' lunches as usual.

"Did you forget your lunch again?" Wendy asked him.

"I didn't forget it. I didn't make one. There wasn't anything good in the refrigerator. Can I have your potato chips, Wendy?"

"Sure." She handed the package over. Jeremy lived on potato chips. Occasionally he ate someone's unwanted apple, but mostly he had chips and pickles for lunch. Honor, who was also across the table, had a faraway look on her face as she slowly ate her sandwich. Wendy thought she looked luscious with her melting brown eyes and her plump lips and caramel skin, but she didn't dare say so. Instead, she said, "That's a pretty blouse, Honor. You look nice."

"Thanks," Honor said and resumed eating. Usually she wore clothes that fit like paper bags over her chunkiness, but today she had on a buttoned checkered blouse that tucked inside her pants, and she looked thinner. Wendy wished she knew what Honor was thinking. If they were friends she could ask, but they weren't so she couldn't.

"I wonder what Meg's doing in Thailand," Wendy said to no one in particular. "I wonder if she's gotten the letters I wrote her yet." No one answered her. Wendy felt as if she were stuck in a telephone booth that was out of order.

"Are you finished with that paper bag?" Jeremy asked her.

"You're not going to eat *that*," the other Sarah said as if she imagined he might.

"Well, actually, I was going to pop it, but I could eat it," Jeremy said eagerly. "Want me to?"

"No!" Wendy said.

"You're a boy, Germy, not a goat. What do you want to wreck your stomach for?" Honor said.

"*I* want you to," the other Sarah said.

Jeremy grinned. He could never resist a dare. Wendy crumpled the bag and tossed it at the garbage can to keep him from getting it. Instead, he tore off a piece of Sarah's bag and ate that.

"You!" the cafeteria aide yelled at Wendy. "Pick up that bag. And you can just stay after lunch and help clean off the tables so you learn not to throw garbage."

Wendy could feel her face reddening from embarrassment. Honor was looking at her pityingly. *Now* she's sorry she's got me in her group, Wendy thought. Why had she been such a fool! Jeremy was telling the cafeteria aide he had to stay and help clean tables too because it was his fault Wendy got in trouble.

"*You* get to class. I've had more than enough of *you*

already this year," the cafeteria aide barked at him.

Honor left without looking back.

*

When Wendy arrived ten minutes late for class, the new girl had already been introduced by Miss Pinelli and was sitting at a desk near the window. She looked like a small blond doll, the kind with thick, fluffy hair that's made to comb and fuss with. "Who is she?" Wendy whispered to Honor while the teacher wrote the language arts assignment on the board.

"Name's Ingrid. Miss Pinelli picked the other Sarah to be her buddy. Poor Ingrid."

A new girl! Wendy couldn't believe it. She'd imagined it happening and it had. Wendy stared at the new girl in awe and said, "She's beautiful, isn't she?" She'd never seen anyone who looked more like a fairy-tale princess.

"I guess," Honor said without interest.

Miss Pinelli gave them the needle eye. "Girls, if one of you wants the assignment explained, raise your hand. There's no need for talking."

Wendy curled up the ends of her long mouth to placate the teacher and started considering a sentence with an active verb in it. Underline the verb. Then write it with a modifying adverb and underline that. Easy. Horses run. Horses run beautifully, Wendy wrote. Out of the corner of her eye, she saw Honor making up a long involved sentence. How was she ever going to find the verb in all that? Well, Honor liked a challenge.

Across the room Ingrid sat with her hands folded looking straight ahead and doing nothing. She's scared, Wendy thought, and yearned to go over, help her get started, and reassure her that Miss Pinelli was strict but decent so long as you behaved yourself. If only she hadn't been out of the room when Miss Pinelli picked a buddy for Ingrid!

Gym was held outdoors in good weather. Today was cloudy and cool which was good enough. Wendy found herself behind Ingrid as they lined up for their turn in the kickball game.

"Do you like kickball?" Wendy asked Ingrid.

"Yes, I like sports," Ingrid said.

"I guess I do too, but I'm not very good at them," Wendy said.

Ingrid said nothing.

"Did you just move here?"

"Yes, from Iowa."

"I bet you feel bad, leaving your friends."

"We lived on a farm. I didn't have friends except in school."

"I never knew anybody who lived on a farm," Wendy said. "What's it like? I mean, what kind of farm?"

"Corn. My father tried pigs too, but that didn't work either."

"That's too bad," Wendy said. "I mean for your father."

"Well, he's working on trucks now and he doesn't mind. He says there's more opportunity in a place like this."

"Opportunity for what?"

"Well, for meeting people."

Wendy smiled, and her heart thumped an extra beat because here she was, a person hoping to be met. "You have such beautiful hair," Wendy said. "I wish I had hair like yours."

"It sticks out," Ingrid said. "I want it to lie flat, but every time I brush it, it sticks out."

"I think you look perfect," Wendy said fervently. She pulled at one of her own curls. It felt sticky. She'd better wash her hair tonight to look her best for Ingrid.

Ingrid was looking at her uneasily. "I'm up," she said and moved purposefully forward. For such a small, delicate-looking girl, she had a powerful kick. Kids cheered her as she ran to first base.

"Way to go . . . Wow . . . What's her name? . . . Ingrid . . . Hey, Ingrid, great kick."

Ingrid paid no attention to her audience. She stood there intent on the next move in the game, ready to dash for second if Wendy's kick was any good. As usual, Wendy bunted the ball. She was twice Ingrid's size, but not half the athlete. Wendy swelled with admiration and a yearning to do things for Ingrid. Without a doubt, Ingrid was the friend she'd been seeking.

"Would you like to come over to my house after school?" Wendy asked her at the water fountain after recess.

"I can't today, but thank you for asking," Ingrid said.

"Tomorrow?"

"Maybe," Ingrid said.

A postcard showing a fancifully decorated elephant was there from Meg when Wendy got home. "We live in the smallest place you ever saw. Everything's a mess, but interesting," Meg had written. Not a very long postcard, but at least it showed Meg was thinking about her. At last everything was going right again.

That night Wendy curled up in bed with Tink and wrote Meg back about the new girl who'd come into their class, "Like I conjured her up because I need her so badly. It's enough to make me believe in magic. . . ." She hoped that when Ingrid and she became good friends, Meg wouldn't be jealous. Probably Meg wouldn't be. Probably she'd be glad. A good friend was glad for you when you got what you wanted. Wendy propped the postcard against the lamp on her night table so she could look at the elephant until she fell asleep.

6

Winning a Friend

Wendy locked her bike into the rack near the side door of the school and couldn't believe her luck. The girl walking toward the glass front door was Ingrid. If Ingrid lived near enough to school to be a walker, she mustn't live too far from Wendy's house, no more than biking distance anyway. "Hi! Hi, Ingrid!" Wendy yelled and waved her arms enthusiastically to get Ingrid's attention.

The doll-like girl turned to see who was calling her. Wendy rushed up to her and said, "Let me carry your books. You're really overloaded."

"I'm okay." Ingrid tried to grasp the door handle with the arm carrying the books. The other hand grasped a lunch box and gym bag.

Wendy reached past her and opened the door. "You really don't need to carry *all* your books home, you know, just what you need for homework."

"My mother wanted to see them," Ingrid said. She dropped a book as she stepped inside.

Wendy scooped it up and begged, "Won't you

please let me carry your books?"

Reluctantly, Ingrid handed them over. Wendy beamed with joy at being of service, but Ingrid didn't smile back. So far the only fault Wendy could see in her was that she seemed awfully serious. "Well, so what did she think?" Wendy asked.

"Who?"

"Your mother, about the books."

"She didn't like a couple of chapters in the science and health book."

"We don't use that much anyway," Wendy said.

Their footsteps echoed in the empty hall as they passed the unlit windows of the office and turned into the long corridor of fifth and sixth grade classrooms. "Are we allowed in the school when nobody's here?" Ingrid asked uneasily.

"Oh, sure. The librarian lets you come in early to sit and read. Or you can join library club and help shelve books before school. I'd do that but my friend Meg—she moved to Thailand last month—well, she didn't want to, and besides, I like to sleep late usually, so—" Wendy halted. Ingrid was staring at a drawing in a bulletin board display labeled, "Emotions." It showed a boy and girl kissing and was called "Love."

"My mother wouldn't like *that*," Ingrid said with conviction.

"Why?" Wendy asked. The boy and girl figures were rounded realistically and pressed against each other. "I wish I could draw that well. That's a pretty talented fifth grader."

"I just hope my mother never sees it. She says you

learn things you shouldn't in public schools. She'd send me to private school, but we can't afford it."

"Well, that's too bad. I mean that you can't afford it, but I'm glad you're going to this school. It's really a good one."

Ingrid looked doubtful as they continued to the library.

The islands of double-sided shelves in the library were packed with books in colorful jackets, and the blue walls were bright with posters. Mrs. Hunt, the librarian, was gray-haired and twinkly. Usually. She sparked instead of twinkling if somebody acted up in her library, or when Germy got interested in volcanoes or airplanes or whales and took out a stack of books he forgot to return. Jeremy lost more books than anyone else in the school. Wendy wondered how his mother managed to pay his library bill at the end of the year. He and his mother and lots of brothers and sisters lived in a trailer, and everyone said they were pretty poor.

Honor and Mrs. Hunt were standing side by side at the card catalogue filing cards. "Hi, Honor. Hi, Mrs. Hunt; this is Ingrid." Wendy made the introductions proudly. "She came to our class just yesterday."

Mrs. Hunt asked Ingrid what she liked to read.

"Animal stories mostly," Ingrid said.

"Wendy can certainly show you where those are. They're her favorites too, aren't they?" Mrs. Hunt smiled at Wendy.

Wendy nodded. "I just read one by Mary Stolz, *Cat Walk*. It was great."

Ingrid picked out three books on horses, and then it was time to go to class. Wendy set the textbooks she was still carrying on Ingrid's desk, then crossed the room to her own desk next to Honor, who had a funny look on her face.

"How come you're carrying her books?" Honor asked.

"Well, just because," Wendy said, and thinking out loud she added, "I wish Ingrid could sit on this side of the room." If Miss Pinelli hadn't moved Jeremy into Meg's old seat, Ingrid would be sitting next to Wendy.

"Do you want me to switch with her?" Honor asked unexpectedly.

"What?"

Honor was looking straight ahead. "I'll move if that's what you want," she said, and added, "I don't care."

Wendy was confused. Why was Honor being so nice to her? Honor was the most complicated girl! One minute she was warm and the next she frosted over. "Well, if you wouldn't mind," Wendy said. "And if Ingrid wants to sit here—"

"Go ask her then," Honor snapped. She looked fierce, as if she were angry at Wendy for some reason.

Miss Pinelli was checking her attendance cards when Wendy went up to her desk and said quickly, "If Ingrid wants to, would you let her sit near me? Honor said she'd move to the window seat."

"Fine," Miss Pinelli said absently.

Ingrid hesitated when Wendy told her about the move. She didn't look too eager, but she finally said, "Well, okay," and picked up her books and her bag. Wendy helped her carry things. They passed Honor lugging her belongings in the opposite direction. Honor ignored them.

"How come Honor moved?" Jeremy asked Wendy after Miss Pinelli told them to stand for the Pledge of Allegiance.

"I don't know," Wendy said. "I guess maybe she wants to sit near the window or something."

"I like Honor," Jeremy said.

"So do I," Wendy told him. "Don't worry. She'll still be in our group, and maybe Ingrid can be in it, too."

That morning they had art instead of gym. Wendy showed Ingrid where the glue pots were and the box of paper scraps they were using for collages.

The art teacher thanked Wendy and said she'd take over now. She bent beside Ingrid to explain.

Honor, who was sitting behind Wendy, said low enough so that just Wendy could hear, "You keep pushing yourself at her and that new kid's going to think you're strange."

Wendy got angry. "I don't need your advice, thanks anyway," she said. She almost added, "especially when you won't even be my friend," but didn't.

Honor blinked and said, "Well, excuse me."

"You really are bossy, Honor," Wendy persisted. "And I'm not as dumb as you think I am." She was amazed to see Honor's face crumple as if she'd been hit.

"It comes from living with my grandmother," Honor mumbled. "She runs the Girls' Home. I probably sound like her."

"Oh, Honor. You sound fine," Wendy assured her guiltily. "And maybe you're right, but—you made me mad."

Honor turned around in her seat and pretended to get absorbed in her art project. "It was very nice of you to let Ingrid sit near me in homeroom," Wendy whispered.

Honor pretended not to hear her.

Wendy looked forward to lunchtime when she could talk to Ingrid and get to know her better. She steered Ingrid to seats near the window in the cafeteria. Jeremy sat down across from them. Honor sat alone on the other side of the room. Wendy suspected Honor was still angry at her. "I'm going to get milk. Do you want any?" Wendy asked Ingrid.

"No, thank you. I have my thermos."

Since Jeremy was lost in a book, Wendy didn't ask him. Besides he had a sandwich with him today. But as she passed by Honor to get to the end of the milk line, Wendy asked, "Want me to get your milk for you?"

"I can get my own."

"Why are you mad at me?" Wendy asked.

"I'm not mad."

"Well, come sit at our table then, okay?"

"I've got some thinking to do."

"Honor, I don't want you to be mad at me," Wendy said.

"You got the friend you wanted," Honor said irritably. "Stop wasting your time on me and go talk with her."

During lunch, Wendy again invited Ingrid to her house after school.

"I can't today," Ingrid said.

"Well, when can you come?"

"I'll have to ask my mother."

"Is your mother *very* strict, Ingrid?"

"I don't know." Ingrid thought about it. Then she said, "When we had the farm, there weren't any kids near us and Mama liked me to help with the canning and the cooking. I had friends in school, but not after."

"That doesn't sound like much fun," Wendy said sympathetically.

"Oh, I had fun. When my big brothers came back to visit, I had fun then. They always played ball with me, even though Mama thinks girls should be girls and—I love playing ball, any kind. I'm good at it."

"Yes," Wendy said, thinking of Ingrid on the field yesterday.

"But I'll ask her if I can visit you. Will your mother be home?"

"Sure, my mother and probably my stepsister and brothers too."

*

Honor accepted Ingrid into their social studies group without comment. All she did was ask Ingrid, "Is your handwriting any good?"

Ingrid's handwriting was small and precise and clear, like Ingrid herself. She seemed glad to be secretary and sat there quietly taking notes while they discussed what was important in the filmstrip they were viewing.

Honor set Jeremy to work drawing illustrations of early tools. Their subject was how early man made a living. Every time Jeremy got sidetracked and started drawing monsters with electrical charges coming out of their heads or airplanes zapping one another in midair, Honor steered him firmly back to what he was supposed to be doing for the group.

"You're going to be a terrific teacher some day," Wendy said.

"I'm going to be a lawyer," Honor said coldly.

After the last bell of the day, Wendy asked Honor if she would be at the playground later. "Why?" Honor asked as they walked out of the school together.

"I just thought maybe we could meet there."

"Isn't Ingrid coming over to your house?"

"Honor, don't be like that. If you wanted, we could all three be friends."

"Two's company, three's a crowd."

"That's not true. Three's more fun sometimes."

"My grandmother, who's the smartest person I know, already told me I was going to be sorry if I messed around with you. And the way you were today, it looks like she was right."

"Why? What did I do? And anyway, your grand-mother doesn't even know me." Wendy was indignant.

"She knows how people are," Honor said, and her plump lips pressed together firmly while her eyes blotted Wendy out.

"Just tell me why you're mad at me," Wendy insisted. "Just tell me."

"I sat next to you all year," Honor blurted out.

"But if you didn't want to move your seat, why did you say you would?" Wendy asked.

"I just wanted to see what you'd say," Honor said. "And you said what I expected."

Wendy was mystified. What was Honor testing her about? Honor had made it plain she didn't want to be a friend, so why should she care who else Wendy made friends with? Honor was a pain. She was just too hard to understand, Wendy decided impatiently as she turned away from her and headed toward the bike stand.

7

Just the Two of Us

The house was quiet when Wendy got home from school. It seemed to be talking to itself in refrigerator hum and clock tick and the sizzling sound of Mother's sewing machine. This was the kind of quiet Wendy remembered coming home to in their old apartment when it was just the two of them. She crept into the sewing room, waited patiently until the end of a seam, then clapped her hands over Mother's eyes. "Boo."

"Wendy, are you home already?"

"Same time as usual. Where is everybody?"

"Chick and Eric went to a friend's house and Ellen's going to her voice lesson right from school."

"Alone at last!" Wendy exulted.

"It has been a long time, hasn't it?" Mother turned to put her slim arms around Wendy for a hug.

"Weeks," Wendy said. "Let's go for a walk in the country, just you and me. Please, Mom."

Mother stretched. "Why not? I'm sick of working,

sick of being indoors. Come on. Let's escape before the phone rings and someone needs me for something."

Wendy grabbed a banana as an after-school snack and they set forth into the caressing spring day. They strolled through two residential streets of small homes, crowded in by big bushes and trees, then crossed the highway to the empty fields they'd discovered last summer. Wendy had christened the fields "the country" because it wasn't a park, the way a place with trees and wild plants and a pond would be in the New York City area. It was free space, and if anybody owned this land, they hadn't fenced it off or built on it or put up signs to keep people out. The only paths had been worn by wanderers like themselves.

"The truth is," Mother mused, "if I were still working for the department store and dealing with earth shattering matters like whether belts are in or out this season, I wouldn't be able to go walking with my darling daughter on the spur of the moment, would I?"

"Do you miss your job?"

"I miss working with people and the excitement a little, but it—no, that's not what bothers me. What bothers me is that I don't feel qualified for full-time motherhood. Four children! And to think my mother raised me to expect a glossy existence without dirty dishes or anyone's underwear but my own." Mother's laugh was rueful.

Wendy took her hand comfortingly. "You're sorry you married Wally?"

"Oh, no. Wally's a dear. It's not him; it's his kids who are driving me mad. Ellen's so needy that I can't do enough to satisfy her, and Chick and Eric are—well, they're not bad kids, but like this morning I went to a parent teacher conference and got laid out by Eric's teacher as if it's all my fault Eric has poor work habits and isn't working up to his potential. She asked if he did his chores around the house, and I had to admit he didn't have any. She told me very pointedly that children learn work habits at home. I felt awful."

"But you haven't even been his mother for a year," Wendy protested.

"Umm," Mother said. "And then on my way out I saw Chick sitting in the principal's office, in trouble again, and no sooner did I get home than I got a phone call from the guidance counselor about Ellen."

"What did she do?"

"I can't tell you. But whatever you do, *don't* use Ellen as a role model."

"You don't like her anymore?"

"Of course, I like her. My heart goes out to the girl. I never saw anyone so hungry for approval."

"Oh," Wendy said.

"What do you mean, 'oh'? Don't you think it's pathetic that she decks herself in those bizarre outfits just to attract attention?"

What Wendy had thought was that Ellen was a show-off. "I guess so," she said.

"Don't get me wrong," Mother said. "I do love my stepchildren. It's just—" Her voice trailed off.

Wendy's spirits sank. She set herself to the task of

finding dainty early spring wildflowers amid the stalks of dead plants, told herself to be glad Mother wasn't thinking of leaving Wally, and finally accused herself of being jealous of Ellen again. She never used to be a jealous person. What had gotten into her? She would have confessed to Mother how she felt, but Mother didn't need another worry right now.

Somehow it seemed that they couldn't talk freely to each other anymore. Mother couldn't tell her about Ellen, and Wendy couldn't say that she sometimes felt like a guest who'd outstayed her welcome in Wally's house.

"Now it's your turn," Mother said. "How's it going for you, puss? Is the new girl warming up?"

Wendy nodded. "Ingrid's coming over tomorrow. You'll be home, won't you?"

"Of course, where else?"

"Her mother's very strict, so it's important," Wendy said, and added, "I don't think Ingrid likes me too much yet."

"Wendy! Why shouldn't she like you?"

"I don't know . . . Ellen thinks I'm a slob. I'm *not* very neat. Ingrid's neat." Wendy looked down at herself. She was wearing a T-shirt that was baggy at the neck. It was half tucked in and half hung over her loose pants. "Is being sloppy bad enough to keep people from liking you?"

"I wouldn't worry about it," Mother said and brushed Wendy's snarl of curls back from her forehead.

Wendy had always been grateful that Mother didn't

nag her about her looks. Now she asked, "Would you like me better if I was neat?"

"I find you altogether lovable," Mother said, "but if you paid more attention to appearance, well, I'd be pleased, of course."

"I bet Tink's the only person in the world who likes me just the way I am," Wendy said.

Mother laughed as if Wendy'd made a joke and crouched over a circlet of large, clover-shaped leaves with pinkish white flowers springing from the center.

"Pretty," Wendy said, leaning on her shoulder.

"I've been thinking, puss," Mother said. "Maybe instead of always relying on just one friend, you'd be better off branching out a little. You ought to join a club or take a class in art or dance the way Ellen does. That way you wouldn't have to depend on your classmates and how they treat you."

"I hate schedules," Wendy said. "Fun's more fun when it's not organized." Mother nodded agreement and Wendy added, "You don't have to worry about me. I'm all right."

They continued walking and Mother said, "I've never worried about you much. You've always been a happy kid who made friends easily. Can you even count the number of birthday parties you've been invited to since nursery school?"

"Best friends are harder though," Wendy said. "Every time I find one, something happens, or she moves away, like Meg. I wish I had just one friend who was always and forever."

"Most people wish that," Mother said. "It's what I married Wally to get, partly anyway." She smiled at Wendy who smiled back.

They arrived at the pond which was the pivot point of their walks. The water was coffee colored and still.

"There's a girl in my class named Honor," Wendy said. "You know—that girl who lives in the garden apartments? She acts as if she doesn't want or need any friends. I don't understand her."

"Some people like being alone."

"But Honor's interested in people, sort of. I mean, she's even nice to Jeremy, and sometimes she's nice to me. It could be she just won't make friends with white kids."

"Maybe she's afraid."

"Of what?"

"Of prejudice."

Wendy considered that. It was hard to imagine Honor afraid of anything. "Remember I told you how she's got white stepbrothers she doesn't like? And she lives with her grandmother who's black," Wendy said. "Do you think Honor's mad because her mother married somebody white?"

"Could be," Mother said. "Is her mother black?"

Startled by Mother's question, Wendy said, "Oh, sure. Honor's black; so her mother has to be."

"Not necessarily," Mother said. "Americans are a mixed batch. Lots of people have several national and racial origins. You're one-sixteenth Cherokee, you know."

"I know," Wendy said. It had been exciting the first time she'd heard it, but not anymore. She tugged at a curl. "Anyway, Honor must be mad at her mother or she wouldn't be living with her grandmother."

"Why don't you ask Honor about it if you're so interested?"

"Oh, I couldn't." She wouldn't dare ask Honor personal questions. "But I bet she feels bad about not being with her mother. I'd feel awful if I didn't live with you."

"I'd feel awful too," Mother said.

Of course, Wendy realized, that was probably why Honor was so moody. She was unhappy and too proud to show it. The thing to do was be more patient with Honor's on-off moods, and maybe someday, when she was in an on mood, Honor might confide in her again.

"I had so hoped you and Ellen would be friends," Mother was saying. "Do you think it's possible that you and she may be a little jealous of each other?"

"Why should Ellen be jealous of *me?*" Wendy asked in amazement. "You spend most of your time fussing over her."

Mother looked pained. "Am I neglecting you, darling?"

"It's okay," Wendy said. "I mean, I know you've got to be mother to everybody now, not just me, and you've got a husband and the dressmaking business— I know how busy you are. Really, I do."

"Oh, Wendy," Mother's green eyes were bright with

feeling as she held Wendy's shoulders and looked into her face. "You must know I love you most of all. *That's* why Ellen could be jealous of you."

A warm wave of pleasure swept through Wendy, buoying her up as she realized that no matter how it had seemed, she and Mother were still close.

They walked home in green twilight time. The sky above the trees was the color of pale grass and the clouds were tinged with pink. A hush lay over everything in a world so beautiful it hurt.

*

Mother tried to make Chick set the table that evening. He said he didn't have to and that Wendy should do it. Mother told him it was his turn. Finally she sent him to his room to think about it. He went, but he slammed the door so hard the whole house shook.

"He probably thinks he can get away with it because Wally's not coming home from his sales trip till Friday," Wendy said.

"Ignore him. He's just a brat," Ellen advised.

"We have to help him control his temper," Mother said, but she didn't sound as if she knew how. At seven-thirty she left for a Parent Teacher Organization meeting which had to do with effective discipline. Wendy hoped it would help.

A while later, Wendy was ironing in the kitchen.

"Are you burning my blouse?" Ellen yelled from the living room where she was watching TV. "I smell something." She zoomed into the kitchen in her pink and purple leotards.

"I'm not burning it."

"You are. Look. You scorched it. I should have known better than to trust a slob like you with my good clothes. You never do anything right."

Wendy was indignant. Ellen knew Wendy was a good ironer or she'd never have let her near her blouse. "It's all right," Wendy said. "See?" She turned the blouse right side out. It was beautifully ironed, and luckily the slight singe that she had indeed allowed to happen on the back didn't show through.

"It's scorched. If it gets a hole next time it's washed, you're going to pay for it."

"Okay, I will." Wendy handed the blouse to Ellen, who stood there quivering with three sparkly purple nails and the brush still in her hand to paint the rest. It occurred to Wendy that Ingrid's mother might not approve of a girl who looked like a rock star.

"Are you going to be home tomorrow afternoon?" Wendy asked cautiously.

"What do you care?"

"I was just wondering. I have a friend coming over."

"So? Don't expect *me* to help you entertain her." Ellen put her leg up backward and dropped her head to meet the sole of her foot, then stretched the other leg the same way and said, "Actually, tomorrow I have to get Mother to take me shopping for a new outfit. I got invited on a picnic by a high school boy."

"She can't tomorrow. She promised to be around while my friend's here. Her mother won't let Ingrid come otherwise."

"Are you serious? What kind of baby is she? Anyway, she can visit you some other day. I have to go shopping."

Wendy didn't say anything. Mother had promised her first and would no doubt keep her word, knowing how important it was to Wendy.

Cookies, Wendy thought. That's what she could do, bake some sugar cookies. Half the recipe should be enough. It would be nice to offer Ingrid something home-baked.

8

Ingrid Comes

Wally arrived home unexpectedly late that night. Deliveries of the medical supplies he sold were being fouled up by the computer, and he wanted to straighten out the problem before seeing any more customers. Hearing his laugh downstairs the next morning, Wendy hurried to the kitchen and found Chick and Eric breakfasting on sugar cookies. "I baked those for my friend!" she cried. Only three cookies remained of the sheetful she'd left cooling on the counter overnight. "You pigs!"

"Dad and Ellen ate some too," Eric said.

Wally looked up from the omelet he was cooking and said, "Sorry, Wendy. I didn't know they were company cookies. You should have put a sign on them."

"Where's Mother?" Wendy asked. She knew her mother would restock the cookie jar rather than leave such a stingy quantity of cookies to serve a guest.

"Your mother's got problems," Wally said. "She

used the wrong material on some lady's collar, and she's been ripping and sewing since dawn. Don't I get a kiss hello?"

She kissed him and asked if *he* had time for cookie buying. "Gee, I'm going to the office and then right back on the road. How about if I bring you some on my return trip Friday?"

"Friday's too late, but thanks anyway," Wendy said.

"There's gingersnaps in the cookie jar," Wally told her.

"Nobody likes them."

"I do," Wally said.

Tinkerboy appeared and gave his feed-me cry. No sooner had Wendy fed him than he cried to be let out.

Mother sagged into a seat at the kitchen table, looking hollow-eyed.

"Are you going to the supermarket this morning, Mom?" Wendy asked. "Can't," Mother said. "Whatever we need has to wait until I get this suit done."

"Delicious," Wally said of the omelet he was sampling. "How can I be so handsome and such a good cook besides?" He slid half the omelet onto a plate for Mother and offered Wendy some of his, but she refused.

Chick and Eric said good-bye, grabbed their lunches, and scooted out the back door on their way to play baseball with friends before school. Suddenly Eric backed up, opened his lunch box and said, "Here, Wendy."

She thanked him for the cookie. That made four. Except when she looked, only two remained on the cookie sheet. "*Now* who ate the cookies I baked for Ingrid?" she demanded indignantly.

Ellen, who had appeared in the kitchen as silently as Tink, said, "Oh, were those for your friend? I'm sorry." She held out the one she'd bitten into as if Wendy could take it back.

Today Ellen was wearing her pink and purple neon with matching bows in her hair. "You're not going to school looking like *that,* are you?" Wally said.

"What's wrong with how I look?" Ellen compressed her wild pink lips and narrowed her purple passion eyelids. Her rouged cheeks burned brightly against the white of her skin and her voice shook as she said, "I spent an *hour* doing my face this morning."

"Well, there's too much glop on it," Wally said. "What's a pretty girl like you need all that paint for?"

"It's in style, Daddy. It's what the magazines show," Ellen said.

"For night club singers or thirteen-year-old girls?"

"Mother!" Ellen appealed.

"It *is* a little overdone," Mother murmured.

Ellen turned on the curved heel of her pink sandal and raced upstairs. They could hear her bawling all the way.

"You can't say anything to that kid these days," Wally said.

"She's at a sensitive age," Mother said.

"Do the girls in her grade *all* look like her?" Wally asked Wendy.

"No," Wendy said honestly, "Ellen just wants to stand out." She did too, like a one-girl theatrical production.

Wally looked anxious. "Relax," Mother said. "I'll see what I can do." She went upstairs. She was still up there when Wendy had to leave for school. She'd meant to remind Mother that she had to be home when Ingrid came that afternoon. Well, it would be all right; Mother was too tired and too busy to go out. As for the cookies, it was possible Ingrid might like gingersnaps. Cookies weren't likely to make or break a friendship anyway.

A carnival of tulips caught Wendy's eye in the yard of the white colonial house on the corner. Red, yellow, white, and purple tulips were bobbing in the wind in every yard she passed now that she looked. Life had to be good when the sky was such a bright blue and even the traffic light was jigging merrily. Before she was halfway to school, Wendy began to whistle.

Jeremy was having a fidgety day and acted up in math. He popped out of his seat as soon as Miss Pinelli began explaining about the review test. She stopped in midsentence and fixed her gaze on him. "Sit down, Jeremy."

"I got to sharpen my pencil."

"When I'm finished talking."

"But then I'll forget."

"I'll remind you."

Jeremy sat. Miss Pinelli continued explaining. Jeremy stood up again. "What now, Jeremy?"

"I gotta go to the bathroom."

Miss Pinelli's voice slurred from annoyance. "Youbetterbeback in five minutes." Jeremy had been known to lose a whole period in the bathroom.

Not today though. The class was working busily when he returned singing "One little, two little, three little Indians. . . ."

"Quiet, Jeremy."

"Sorry, Miss Pinelli. Some first graders were singing in the bathroom and I caught it from them."

"That will do, Jeremy."

He shut up and tiptoed to his seat with exaggerated motions that caused some titters. Even Honor smiled. Ingrid didn't. She was concentrating hard on the math assignment.

"Jeremy!" Miss Pinelli said.

"Do you want me, Miss Pinelli?" Eagerly he snapped to attention.

"Just sit down and get to work."

Jeremy sat. He didn't have a pencil as usual. He looked through his book bag and papers and desk. Finally Wendy gave him one of hers. "Thanks, Wendy," he said, and added warmly "Gee, you're nice to me."

Kids turned to grin at Wendy slyly. Even Honor was looking. Wendy blushed. It was risky to be nice to Jeremy in a quiet room. Next they'd start teasing her about being his girlfriend. She bent her head to her paper. Ingrid worked on diligently.

Jeremy waved his hand in the air. "Um, Miss Pinelli!"

Miss Pinelli cringed. "Now what?"

"What are we supposed to be doing?" More suppressed laughter.

"It's on the board, Jeremy."

He squirmed in his seat. Then he got up. Miss Pinelli moaned. Jeremy said in a hurt voice, "You said I could sharpen my pencil without asking."

"Do it!" Miss Pinelli yelled and Ingrid was so startled that she jumped.

Jeremy sharpened his pencil. He studied the point. Apparently it wasn't sharp enough. He sharpened it some more and reexamined it. By the time Miss Pinelli grabbed him around the neck and walked him back to his desk, he only had half a pencil left. It was sharp though. Miss Pinelli found the right page in the math book and an empty sheet of paper in Jeremy's clutter of a notebook. She pointed to the first example and he got to work.

Wendy finished her page. She noticed that Jeremy was drawing a maze. Honor was marking papers for Miss Pinelli. Ingrid was still working; her lips moved as she counted. The ginger cookies would be good with vanilla ice cream, Wendy thought, and after their snack, she and Ingrid could play a game—whatever game Ingrid liked. Wendy had more than a dozen. She and Meg had loved board games. They'd played them for hours at a time and talked and talked and talked.

Well, today she and Ingrid would play and talk. They'd match up things they had in common and collect understandings the way birds build a nest from twigs and grass. Then, even after Ingrid left to go home, the nest would remain.

At lunch there were boys at Marcy's table, all at one end, but still, they were talking back and forth with Marcy's group. It figured, Wendy thought, that Marcy's group would be the first to start mixing with boys. Honor was sitting with Hee Chung and Dorothy. Wendy wondered if Honor was deliberately avoiding her and why. She wished Honor would say what was wrong. Not knowing why someone was mad at you was awful. Ingrid sat next to Wendy but she was doing workbook pages, trying to catch up. Wendy's mouth felt dry from not talking to anyone.

Eventually the clock read two-thirty.

"Did you walk?" Wendy asked Ingrid as they left the school.

"Yes. I don't have a bike."

"Well, how about sitting on the handlebars of my bike and I'll ride you home?"

"No, that's okay. I'll walk it. How far is it?"

"About eight blocks. Come on, let me ride you. I can do it easy."

Ingrid looked doubtful, but she said, "Well, all right, if you're sure."

Wendy was sure. She'd never ridden a bike with anyone sitting on the handlebars before, but she'd seen other kids do it. "Too bad it's not a boy's bike.

That would be easier," she said. Ingrid boosted herself agilely from the front wheel onto the handlebars and they set off.

Honor stopped walking to watch them. Wendy yelled, "See you, Honor," but Honor just turned away. It was a little harder to pedal with Ingrid aboard, but not too hard. What was difficult was that lampshade of flyaway blond hair. Wendy had to lean to one side or the other of it to see what was ahead. That was how she came to think she was crossing the street on the slant of someone's driveway, when instead she went over the curb just as a car turned the corner. Wendy bumped down hard and Ingrid flew off the handlebars and landed face down in the street.

The car swerved and stopped. A frightened-looking lady got out. "Did I hit her?"

"No, she just fell," Wendy said, choking with guilt. She knew she'd caused the accident.

The lady helped Ingrid up. Ingrid said she was fine, but the scrape on her forehead the size of a belt buckle didn't look fine.

"Better get her home and put ice on that or it'll make a terrible lump," the lady said.

Apologizing all the way, Wendy walked the bike and Ingrid the last two blocks to Wally's little white clapboard house with the green shutters and detached garage. "I'm so sorry. I'm such a clumsy ox. I could kill myself. Do you hurt much, Ingrid?"

"I'm okay," Ingrid said. "It's just a bump." She looked very pale.

"You're so brave!" Wendy cried. What a girl Ingrid was to look so beautiful and be so brave.

"Mother, I'm home. Ingrid's here," Wendy called toward the sound of the sewing machine.

"Just a few minutes and I'll come say hello, darling." Mother sounded as harried as she had this morning.

Ingrid sat at the kitchen table which was covered with a blue vinyl tablecloth. In the middle were napkins in a wooden holder Chick had made in cub scouts and a ceramic salt and pepper shaker Ellen had made in art. Wendy looked for the cold pack Mother had used on Chick just last week and found it in the freezer.

Ingrid sat patiently while Wendy dabbed at the bloody scrape with a gauze pad sprayed with antiseptic. Doing something helpful for Ingrid made Wendy feel better. "Now, hold the cold pack in place over the gauze pad, and I'll get you something to eat," she said.

Ingrid didn't want the gingersnaps even with vanilla ice cream. She didn't want sugar cookies either. She drank a glass of milk and ate a half an apple, but refused the cheese and raisins Wendy offered her to go with the apple. "What do you like to eat?" Wendy asked anxiously.

"I don't eat much," Ingrid said. "Aren't you going to have anything?"

Wendy had forgotten she was hungry. She ate two of her three sugar cookies while Ingrid sat quietly waiting for whatever came next. Wendy stopped eating to ask, "What are your brothers like?"

It was the right question. Ingrid began happily, "Well, the youngest one's nineteen. He taught me how to drive the tractor. The oldest is twenty-seven. He got divorced and Mother wouldn't let him come back home because she doesn't believe in divorce. Besides, she said I was spending too much time with my brothers." Ingrid sighed. "I like boys."

"You do?"

"Well, not as *boyfriends,* just as friends. Because I like outdoor things the way boys do."

"You don't like board games?"

"You mean chess and checkers?"

"Well, I've got Clue and Monopoly and Life and Parcheesi and Scrabble and lots more—I love board games. Or we could play cards."

Ingrid looked uncomfortable. "See, my mother doesn't believe in gambling. Mostly I play outside . . . we could watch television."

Wendy thought not. "There's nothing good on in the afternoon. Tell you what. We can say hi to my mother and then go across the backyard to the playground. How's that?"

"Good." Ingrid cheered up immediately. She left the cold pack on the sink and refused to have the scrape bandaged.

Wendy introduced Ingrid to Mother, saying, "See what I did to her."

Mother was wearing a skirt and a red cotton sweater. She looked pretty, and Wendy was proud of her as she listened sympathetically to the story of how Ingrid had gotten hurt. "Would you girls like to go to the mall this afternoon?" Mother asked then.

"What for?" Wendy asked.

"Well, you could window shop and I'll treat you to sundaes in the ice cream parlor."

"I can't," Ingrid said. "My mother expects to pick me up here at five."

"Oh, I can drop you off at your house," Mother said. "Why don't I just call your mother and ask if that's okay?"

"She isn't home. She works at a bakery."

"We could call her there," Wendy said.

"You said we were going to the playground," Ingrid said stubbornly.

Mother studied Ingrid's expression and said, "I don't think Ingrid really wants to go to the mall." She hesitated, then asked Wendy, "How about if I just run Ellen over to get what she wants and return in an hour? I'll certainly be back before Ingrid's mother comes at five."

"But we said you'd be here," Wendy said.

"Ellen was so upset this morning, Wendy. The only way I could get her calmed down enough to go to school was to say I'd take her to the mall. If you're going to be at the playground, I won't be with you anyway, will I?"

Wendy was hurt that Mother would be so devious for Ellen's sake. She was close to tears as she said, "If you're not back by five, I'll never forgive you."

"Wendy!" Mother said in shock.

Even Ingrid looked at Wendy with surprise. "Come on, let's go," Wendy said. She was angry at her mother, but there was no point in showing it any more than she already had in front of this new friend. An old friend would have understood that Wendy never stayed angry at anybody for long, certainly not her beloved mother.

The door flew open and there was Chick and Eric. "Hi, what's to eat?"

"What happened to baseball practice?" Mother asked.

"They cancelled it cause the coach got sick," Chick said.

Mother pressed her fingers to her temples. "Now what am I going to do?" she asked herself.

With the first enthusiasm she'd shown, Ingrid suggested, "We could take them to the playground to play ball. That would be fun."

"Can you pitch?" Chick asked Ingrid suspiciously.

"Sure," Ingrid said and grinned at the doubt on his face. "Get me a ball and bat and I'll prove it."

Mother sighed with relief. "I'm sorry," she whispered to Wendy. "I'll make it up to you later, puss."

Wendy felt trapped. She followed Ingrid and Chuck and Eric across the backyard toward the open area next to the playground. Ingrid was a couple of inches taller than Eric and about the same size as Chick. Except for her hair, she looked like a boy from the back, Wendy thought. She hoped Ingrid didn't turn out to be *too* much of a tomboy.

"Wendy can't pitch straight," Chick was telling Ingrid. "She can't hit either."

"She bakes good cookies though," Eric said. Wendy

had to smile at him for that. He smiled back secretly.

It took only about five minutes for Ingrid to impress Chick and Eric.

"That's some fastball!" Chick said admiringly.

Wendy sat on a swing and watched. When it was her turn to bat, Chick kept telling her how to stand and how to swing. She tried and missed every ball except one that she bunted. "Well, how am I supposed to hit the ball with you yelling instructions at me?" she asked Chick, who began making fun of her. She returned to her swing in disgust. Boring, she thought. But the other three weren't bored. Ingrid really did like boys best, Wendy thought.

The afternoon was passing quickly. It began to look as if the leisurely talking Wendy had looked forward to so much wasn't going to happen. "Let's go back now. Okay?" Wendy said.

"Is it getting close to five o'clock?" Ingrid stopped pitching to ask.

"I don't know, but you won't have time to see my room or anything if we don't go back soon."

Reluctantly Ingrid called off the ball practice, and the four of them returned through the playground, now full of mothers with their toddlers. "Do you like to read, Ingrid?" Wendy asked.

"Only if there's nothing else to do," Ingrid said.

"Well, what do you like besides playing ball?"

"Horses," Ingrid said.

"Oh, me too." At last, something they had in common!

Mother's car wasn't in the driveway. Wendy felt uneasy when she saw that it was past four. "Is your mother going to be really mad that my mother isn't supervising us?"

"Yes, if your mother's not here," Ingrid said.

"Oh, Mother will be here."

"I like your brothers," Ingrid said.

"Thanks," was the only thing Wendy could think of to reply.

"Any cookies left?" Chick asked.

"You ate your share this morning," Wendy said.

"No, I didn't." Eric and Chick began rummaging through the pantry.

"Come on up to my room," Wendy said to Ingrid. "I have lots of horse books. Oh, and I have a fantastic poster. I got it for my birthday last May." Her birthday was coming around again soon. Suppose she had a birthday party and invited Ingrid. . . .

The poster of the running stallion was set in the closet door so that the molding made a frame around it. Ingrid looked at it and said, "When I grow up, I'd like to be a jockey."

"Um, me too, but I guess I'll be too big. You can be the jockey and I'll be the horse trainer."

She was only being fanciful, but Ingrid shook her head and said seriously, "My mother'd never let me. She doesn't let me do anything much that I really like. I wish I were a boy. Boys get to do the best things. And if I were a boy, I'd be bigger. I *hate* being small."

"But you're so beautiful," Wendy said. "Most girls would give anything to look like you."

"Well," Ingrid said. "I guess for a girl I look okay."

She turned toward Wendy's mirror and frowned hard at her reflection.

On an impulse, Wendy untacked the horse poster from her closet door and told Ingrid, "This is for you."

"Oh, no. I couldn't take your poster."

"But I want you to have it," Wendy said.

They had a silly argument that went, "no, please, no, please," until Ingrid reluctantly accepted the poster and rolled it up to carry home. Just then the doorbell rang.

"Uh oh," Wendy said. She hadn't heard her mother come in, and her mother wasn't likely to be the one ringing the front doorbell. Wendy and Ingrid looked wide-eyed at each other and hurried downstairs. The boys were cutting up newspapers in the middle of the living room floor.

"Some lady's at the door," Eric said.

"Why didn't you let her in?"

"Didn't know who it was."

Wendy opened the door with Ingrid standing beside her. "Hi, Ma," Ingrid said to the tall, stern-eyed lady in a white uniform dress with a hair net flattening her gray hair.

Immediately Ingrid's mother asked her, "What happened to you?"

Ingrid touched her own forehead. "It's nothing. I fell and Wendy put a cold pack on it."

Ingrid's mother surveyed the living room, taking in the newspaper-littered floor, the boys, and Tink, who was cleaning himself on top of the cocktail table. Her face darkened with distaste. "Where is your mother?" she asked Wendy.

"She'll be right back. She just had to run to the store." Wendy twisted her hands and gestured helplessly. "Won't you sit down? She'll be here any minute."

"How long have you children been alone?"

"Well, just a—we were at the playground and—"

Ingrid's mother turned on Ingrid angrily, saying, "You told me her mother would be home." Without waiting for a response, she took Ingrid's arm and told Wendy, "We're leaving now."

"I had a nice time, Wendy," Ingrid said as she was whisked out the door.

Wendy picked up Tink and carried him upstairs to her room. She couldn't remember a time in her life when Mother had failed her this badly. Even when she hadn't picked Wendy up at the baby-sitter's on her way home from work once, it was only because she'd been stalled in an elevator.

Tink purred under Wendy's chin, making comforting vibrations of affection against her throat. "I guess you're going to be my only friend, Tink," Wendy told him. He wouldn't mind that, but she would.

A few minutes later Mother knocked on her door and came in. "The boys told me Ingrid's mother picked her up early," Mother said. "That's bad luck, Wendy. I'm really sorry. What's their number? I'll call and explain."

"Why were you so late?"

"I wasn't. It's only twenty of five. I told you, Ingrid's mother got here early."

"But you shouldn't have gone. You said you'd be here, and you knew how important it was to me, and you went because of Ellen. You say you love me best, but you don't really."

"Wendy, please! I'm trying so *hard* and I'm not pleasing anybody. I feel awful." Mother began to cry. Her crying was quiet, but seeing the tears melted Wendy's anger. It reminded her of long ago when her father had died.

"Don't cry," Wendy told her. "Don't cry. It's okay. If Ingrid's mother won't let her come anymore, we'll still be friends in school. She likes playing with boys better anyway. It's okay, Mom."

"I feel so guilty," Mother said. Her voice quivered. "Darling, I know I'm not doing right by you lately, but it isn't that I don't love you. You can't believe that. It's just that I'm being pulled to pieces."

Mother's unhappiness alarmed Wendy. All at once her problems shrank in size. "Don't worry," Wendy said, "Mom, don't worry. It's okay." Tink got squeezed in their hug. He gave an indignant cry and stalked out of the room.

"Mother!" Ellen called from downstairs.

"Do you forgive me?" Mother asked Wendy.

"Sure," Wendy said. And to prove it she even went downstairs and helped get dinner ready while Mother went to see what Ellen wanted.

9

Jeremy Wants to Come

It was a sad, dim day full of sifting rain. Wendy hoped the weather wasn't an omen. She got to school early, anxious to hear what Ingrid's mother had said about Wendy's mother not being home yesterday afternoon, but Ingrid wasn't there yet. Honor was in the library with Mrs. Hunt. Since she had nothing else to do, Wendy offered to help Honor shelve books.

"So how did it go with Ingrid?" Honor asked. They were working on fiction, with Honor doing the M's to Z's and Wendy handling the first part of the alphabet.

"Pretty good. We played ball."

"Looked to me as if she was having more fun than you," Honor said.

"How do you know?"

"I could see you playing from my bedroom window. That's where I sit to read."

"You should have come down," Wendy said.

"What for? You didn't need me when you had her to have fun with."

"Well, but—" Wendy's eye was caught by a book jacket picture of a skinny, awkward boy who looked like Jeremy. "There's more to being friends than just having fun, Honor."

"Really," Honor said sarcastically. She nodded at the book jacket that Wendy was showing her and agreed it could be Jeremy, then asked, "So what more is there in your opinion?"

"Being there for each other," Wendy said promptly as she tucked the book into place on the shelf.

"I'll tell you what I think's important," Honor said. "Trust. You have to know a friend's not going to betray you. Like that Marcy. You could never trust her to stick with you unless you had something she wanted."

Something in Honor's certainty made Wendy ask, "Have you ever been betrayed?"

"Yes, but not by a friend. I'm careful who I make friends with."

So far as Wendy knew, Honor was so careful she kept everybody at a distance, but that was too hurtful a thing to mention. Instead, Wendy said, "What I'd most like a best friend to be is always and forever." She was thinking of Meg who'd moved out of reach, and her friends in Brooklyn who had closed the circle without her as if she'd never been in it and rarely wrote or called her now.

"Always and forever?" Honor mused. "Nothing's

that, not even this earth. God maybe. . . ."

"I know, but—I guess I just mean that I want a friendship that lasts. Something to really count on."

"You're a dreamer," Honor said. She shook her head and added, "Anyway, you try too hard. Reminds me of a plant I had. I fussed over it so much I watered and fertilized it to death. My grandmother, she has the same kind of plant and she neglects it but hers is beautiful." Honor snorted in disgust. "There I go again, giving advice you don't want."

"That's okay," Wendy said. She was pleased that Honor didn't seem to be angry at her anymore.

"I guess I'm just a naturally bossy person," Honor said as if it bothered her. "I really do take after my grandmother."

"You're smart and you like to straighten people out. There's nothing wrong with that," Wendy said to comfort her.

The first bell rang then and the two girls started to class. Their talk had made Wendy feel so close to Honor that it seemed natural to ask her, "If my mother lets me have a birthday party, will you come?"

"Sure, if I'm not going somewhere else."

"Well, it's the next to last Saturday in May. Save the afternoon, okay?"

Honor smiled in agreement. She had a gorgeous smile.

Ingrid came in during homeroom, neatly dressed in pale blue pants and a matching blue shirt. "Hi, Wendy," she said and sat down.

"Was your mother mad?" Wendy asked. "My mother said she couldn't tell when she called her to explain because your mother didn't say much on the phone."

"I told Ma it wasn't your fault."

"Well, can you come today then?"

"The thing is, I can't invite you back unless my mother's home and she works, so—"

"That's okay," Wendy said quickly.

"Well, I'll see," Ingrid said.

It was still raining outside, but Wendy felt as if she were basking in sunshine because Ingrid's mother hadn't vetoed their friendship after all.

Marcy and Sarah stopped by to ask Ingrid about the scrape on her forehead. Ingrid said she'd fallen without mentioning Wendy's part in it. "Do you want to be on our kickball team after school on Thursdays, Ingrid?" Marcy asked.

"Okay," Ingrid said. "If my mother lets me stay."

"Where do you live? My mother could drive you home," Sarah said.

"That's okay. I can walk," Ingrid said.

So Thursdays Ingrid would be busy, Wendy thought. Well, there were six other days in the week when they could see each other.

At lunchtime, Wendy didn't have to ask. Ingrid just naturally sat down beside her. As usual, she was silent. To entertain her, Wendy began telling about the book she was reading, how the dog in it goes blind but the child who owns him won't give him up. "It's just the most beautiful story," Wendy said. "I cried so hard I could hardly stop."

"How come you have a cat instead of a dog?" Ingrid asked.

"I like cats. Tinkerboy's great company. At night he snuggles against me and purrs like a motorboat. Of course, I like dogs too. Wally, my stepfather, says we can have one. But only if the boys will take care of it because Mother has enough to do as it is. Do you have any pets, Ingrid?"

"Mother won't let animals in the house. But we had a dog outside I liked a lot, and barn cats. That dog could catch just about anything I threw for him. We had to give him away when we left Iowa."

"I'm sorry," Wendy said sympathetically.

Ingrid nodded. "He was a good dog."

She didn't sound very sad about it, Wendy thought, but then Ingrid didn't seem to show emotion. Of course, not showing it didn't mean she didn't feel it. Wendy looked at Ingrid doubtfully.

Honor was sitting at the other end of the table talking to Marcy and Sarah today. From her conversation with Honor in the library, Wendy guessed Honor wanted to be friendly to everyone, without getting close enough so anyone could hurt her. It would be lonely not to be close to anyone, Wendy thought. She'd rather risk getting hurt.

"Marcy invited me over to her house tomorrow," Ingrid said. "If my mother says I can go, I have to bring a note so I can ride the bus. Do you think I need the number of the bus on the note?"

Wendy's heart skipped a beat. "I think so," she said and asked anxiously, "Are you coming over to my house today?"

"Not today," Ingrid said vaguely. This morning she hadn't been sure. Now she was sure. She doesn't like me much yet, Wendy guessed. Probably being a bad ball player and liking cats had put Ingrid off her. Wendy didn't want to be a phony and pretend to be who she wasn't, but what if Ingrid didn't like who she was? What then? Wendy brooded about it in silence. Outside the rain was still coming down.

Lunch was half over when Jeremy appeared with a tray and asked, "Can I sit by you?"

"There's no room," Ingrid said.

"Sure there is," Jeremy said. "Just shove over a little."

Ingrid didn't budge. She glowered at Jeremy, looking quite threatening for such a dainty girl. His tray tilted dangerously, and a dish of macaroni salad bombed her. Gooey noodles spattered Ingrid, the table, and the floor.

"I'm sorry," Jeremy said. "Gee, I'm sorry, Ingrid."

"Just go away and leave me alone, you goofball," Ingrid snapped.

Wendy ran to the lunchroom aide to get a sponge and ran back to wipe up the mess. By the time she'd finished mopping up, lunch was over. Ingrid was still fuming later in the girl's room where Wendy was helping wash the greasy stains from her light blue summer pants. "That boy is such a pest," Ingrid said. "How come you let him hang around you?"

"Jeremy's a good kid, just a little antsy."

"A *little* antsy. Well, if he's your friend—"

"Oh, he's not my friend," Wendy assured her hastily. She certainly didn't want to risk being rejected for associating with him. Jeremy wasn't a friend, just someone for whom Wendy felt sorry because he meant well and was so out of sync.

Bicycling home bareheaded in the drizzle that afternoon, Wendy tried to remember if she'd ever felt as unsure of Meg as she did of Ingrid. She wondered if she could be fertilizing and watering Ingrid too much as Honor had hinted. Could too much eagerness put Ingrid off? It wouldn't put her off, Wendy thought. She'd love it if someone showed they really wanted to be her friend. Strange that friendship was turning out to be her worst subject when she'd thought it was her best.

*

Every night Wendy and Ingrid had a half hour phone call. Half an hour was the limit Ingrid's mother set. Usually when Ingrid called Wendy, it was because she needed to ask Wendy something about homework. Ingrid's mother wanted her to catch up with the workbooks in language arts and science (except for chapters on human development and reproduction) because Ingrid hadn't used those texts in Iowa. Besides, Ingrid's mother believed in homework, and they weren't getting much this late in the spring. Miss Pinelli only assigned a little math and a book report every two weeks, unless they had to review for a test.

When she wasn't doing homework, Ingrid seemed to watch a lot of television. She and Marcy and Sarah were always talking about TV programs they'd seen, unless they were talking about baseball or boys. Wendy was surprised that Ingrid's mother wasn't stricter about TV viewing. Most times when Wendy invited Ingrid over, Ingrid said she was busy. When it turned out Ingrid was busy seeing other people, like Marcy and Sarah, Wendy tried not to be jealous. Having several best friends was good. That was how it had been for Wendy in Brooklyn. She wished she had the chance again and tried not to begrudge it to Ingrid.

Anyway, Wendy had her birthday party to offer Ingrid as a treat. Then Ingrid would see her at her best. She was good at playing hostess and helping people enjoy themselves.

Days when Ingrid did come to her house, Wendy either borrowed Ellen's bike for Ingrid to ride, or took her to the playground, or they played with Chick and Eric who thought Ingrid was neat. Boys were drawn to her. In fact, one of the boys at Marcy's lunch table had a crush on her. Wendy admired how Ingrid ignored the teasing she got about that. Of course, Wendy walked to school if Ingrid was coming home with her so that they wouldn't have another accident doubling up on the bike. On the way home, she usually carried Ingrid's books.

"What do you have to carry her books for?" Honor

asked as she and Wendy sat alone together in the shade of the building during recess one hot sunny afternoon while Ingrid and the rest of the class were playing ball.

"I like to do things for her," Wendy said.

"But it's like you're her servant or something," Honor said.

"I don't think you like Ingrid," Wendy observed.

"She's your friend, not mine," Honor said.

"But why don't you like her?"

"Well, for one thing, she's boring."

"I don't think so," Wendy said loyally. "She just doesn't say much."

"And she hardly ever smiles."

"So, she's serious."

"And she acts like a cold fish."

Wendy was sorry she'd asked. She resented that Honor, who wasn't her friend, should be so critical of Ingrid who was.

*

Mother thought five people would be a good number to invite to the party, but the week before it, Wendy had given out only two invitations. She decided to ask Honor and Ingrid who they'd like her to have.

"Just because she said five doesn't mean you have to have five," Honor said. "Small parties are nice." She looked at her invitation which said lunch and miniature golf. "I like miniature golf," Honor said. "Not that I'm good at it, but I like all the little buildings."

"Me too," Wendy said. "I bet I get a worse score

than you do. The first time I played I got the worst score you could get."

Honor laughed. "We'll have a competition, you and me. No chance Ingrid, the athlete, can beat us for worst."

Ingrid accepted her invitation with thanks. She, too, said she liked miniature golf. Wendy had expected she would. That was why she'd picked it when Mother had given her a choice of miniature golf or a movie.

In class their group was figuring out how to present their charts and reports about how early man got his food. The other Sarah was out sick as usual. Wendy's mind wandered. She hadn't been thinking of much for days except her coming party. Casually she asked Ingrid who else Ingrid wanted her to invite to the party.

"Sarah and Marcy are nice," Ingrid said.

Wendy shook her head. She'd thought about inviting them for Ingrid's sake and decided she shouldn't because they'd made it so plain they didn't like Wendy much. "How about Hee Chung? She's shy, but very nice," Wendy said.

"But she hangs out with Dorothy, and I hate Dorothy."

"You do? Why?"

"Because. I just do."

"Hey, what about me?" Jeremy asked. He was doing the paste-up of pictures from a *National Geographic* article on a chart. And he was being very careful too, maybe because Ingrid had threatened to kick him black and blue if he messed up their work. "Can't I come to your party?"

"It's just girls, Jeremy."

"That's okay. I don't mind."

"Well, we do," Ingrid said rudely.

Jeremy didn't say anything then, but later while Ingrid was off helping Honor get their display boards hung up on the wall, he said to Wendy, "I didn't mean to dump my tray on her that time. It just happened."

"I know," Wendy said.

"I guess she doesn't like me much. Nobody does. I never got invited to a birthday party in my whole life."

Wendy felt so bad for him that she said impulsively, "You can come to mine if you want. *I* like you. I think you're a really nice boy."

He beamed at her. "You mean it?"

"Sure," she said, and to prove it, she got out the leftover invitations and made one out to Jeremy then and there. He carried it off like a prize.

That evening Wendy was watching Tinkerboy bat a wrapped sour ball around the kitchen floor while she talked on the phone with Ingrid. Ellen was dancing in the living room to the MTV station. Mother and Wally were discussing finances at the kitchen table. Eric and Chick were catching bugs on the screen door. In the midst of all those distractions, Wendy was trying to explain to Ingrid how it had happened that she'd given Jeremy an invitation to the party. "It was so sad when he said that about nobody ever inviting him. Isn't that the saddest thing you ever heard?"

"No," Ingrid said. "The reason he never got invited is because he's such a goofball everybody hates him."

"Well, but—"

"I don't know if my mother will let me go to your party if Jeremy is coming," Ingrid warned.

"Your mother doesn't know Jeremy," Wendy pointed out.

Ingrid hesitated, then took a different tack. "I've told her about him. Anyway, you think it over." And she repeated, "I don't think I can come if Jeremy does." Next she said good-bye and hung up.

Wendy was stunned. How had she gotten herself into such a predicament? Because of Jeremy who wasn't even a friend of hers, that's how. What good was a birthday party if her only possible best friend wouldn't attend? No good. No good at all.

Tink playfully bit her bare toe. Wendy jumped and cried, "Tink!" She gathered the cat up and carried him to her room. She wanted to lie down and get some comfort from him as she thought about how she was going to manage to glue her birthday party together again.

10

Pleasing People

Ellen's yelling woke Wendy up on Saturday morning, but she wouldn't have rolled out of bed and rushed downstairs if she hadn't heard her mother yelling back. Mother never yelled. Barefoot and still in her pajamas, Wendy arrived at the kitchen just as Ellen slammed out the door. Mother flew past Wendy on her way through the living room toward her bedroom. It used to be the dining room but it had been turned into a master bedroom for Mother and Wally.

"Mom, what's going on?"

Mother stopped short of banging into the cocktail table and looked wild eyed at Wendy. "Nothing," she quavered. "Nothing. Just Ellen being her usual impossible self." Then Mother did something really strange. She picked up a movie magazine Ellen had left on the floor and, gritting her teeth, tried to rip it in half.

"Mother, that's Ellen's!"

Mother tossed the magazine at the couch and

slumped into an armchair. "I can't stand it anymore," she said. "I thought the fashion world was high pressure, but this is worse. Come hug me, puss. I'm in a bad way."

Wendy balanced on the arm of the chair and gave her mother a good hugging. "What did Ellen do?"

"It's not what she's done. It's what she wants to do. She wants to go off with this high school boyfriend of hers for the weekend. She says a whole group of kids are going to somebody's camp at the lake and that some of them are eighteen. Hence they don't need a chaperone. I told her no way was I allowing her to do that. You know what she said? She said, 'If you were my real mother, you'd trust me.' I could have killed her!"

"Call Wally. He's her real father."

"I can't reach him. He's off at a sales conference for the day."

"When's he coming home?"

"Not until dinner. She'll be gone by then if I haven't managed to stop her. She only listens to me when I'm giving her what she wants. What am I supposed to do, knock her down and tie her up?" Mother sounded bitter.

"You could call the boy's mother."

"I could, couldn't I? Good idea, Wendy. Better yet, I'll go over there. That may be where she went anyway." Mother gave Wendy a kiss and said soberly, "I don't know what I'd do without you. You're my sanity." Then she jumped up and grabbed her handbag, but as she was leaving, she called over her shoulder, "Watch the boys for me till I come back?" She didn't wait for an answer.

Uh oh, Wendy thought. Up to that instant, the big problem in her life this morning had been how to gently uninvite Jeremy. Now she had Chick and Eric to deal with, too.

A faint mewling sound alerted her. She dashed upstairs. Her stepbrothers were in the bathroom and so, apparently, was Tinkerboy.

"Let me in," Wendy demanded when the door wouldn't open. It made her angry that they were still playing pranks on her. She'd thought they'd given up on the teasing and started accepting her as part of their family. She had even begun to like them.

"Open this door," she commanded, rattling the doorknob.

Of course it was Eric who obeyed.

Chick was trying to hold Tinkerboy in the bathtub. The cat was soapy and wet and so was Chick. "What are you doing to my cat?" Wendy screeched.

"Nothing, just washing him," Chick said.

"We thought he'd get sick licking the glue off, Wendy," Eric said.

"Glue?"

"He was on the chair when the bottle rolled off the table," Chick said. "Wanna help us rinse him off? He's kind of hard to hold with only four hands."

It sounded reasonable. Wendy calmed down and they finished bathing Tinkerboy together. She dried him with her own towel which she then dumped in the wash. Tink showed his dissatisfaction with their work by promptly rebathing himself with his tongue.

"What were you doing with the glue?" Wendy thought to ask.

"Making you a birthday present," Eric said.

She eyed them suspiciously.

"Your birthday's next Saturday. Mother said," Chick insisted.

"Show me the present."

"Now? Then it won't be a surprise."

"You better show it to me or you'll be in trouble for messing with my cat." She was proud of how tough she sounded. Mother might not have learned how to deal with her stepchildren, but Wendy had. What they showed her was a box with horse pictures glued all over it.

"That's a neat present," she said, "but where'd you get the pictures?"

"From a magazine." Chick looked hard at Eric. Eric folded in his lips.

"Where'd you get the magazine?"

"We bought it," Chick said virtuously, a little too virtuously.

Wendy didn't quite believe him but decided it wouldn't pay to look a gift horse in the mouth, especially one in the shape of a box. She could use it for special keepsakes, like the postcard from Meg and the scattered letters from her old friends in Brooklyn and special birthday and valentine cards.

"Did you eat breakfast yet?" she asked.

"No, Mother was too busy yelling at Ellen to make us any. Ellen's a pain," Chick said.

"So are you sometimes," Wendy told him cheerfully. "Want me to make you some French toast?"

"Okay," Chick agreed. "You do that good."

While Wendy was contentedly making the boys their French toast, the solution to her party problem flashed in her head. It was simple. She would disinvite Jeremy by telling him the party had turned into a sleepover. Even Jeremy would understand he couldn't come to a girls' sleepover. The only difficulty would be priming Honor and Ingrid to say "sleepover" if they happened to mention the party in school.

Ingrid might not be willing to lie, even to tell a white lie to save Jeremy's feelings. For that matter, Honor might not either. Actually, Wendy wasn't all that good about white lies herself. She tended to blush. Well then, what she could do was to really change the party to a sleepover. But where would they all sleep? The house was packed full as it was, and with Chick and Eric around, it would be a disaster. End of the flashed solution.

Tink followed Wendy upstairs and meowed from the window sill while she got dressed. He wanted out. "Half a minute till I throw on some clothes," Wendy told him. It didn't take her much longer than that to let Tink out the back door. The boys were playing in their sandpile, constructing a new highway with dump trucks and a concrete mixer.

Wendy settled onto the back doorstep to think.
Over by the garage, a clump of white irises looked like
stalky orchids now that they were beginning to
flower. Next week, if the irises were still blooming,
she could decorate her birthday party table with them
or give each guest one to take home. As for Marcy
and Sarah, why not invite them to her party as long
as Ingrid liked them so much? So what if they didn't
like Wendy enough to ever invite her back.

Suddenly Chick gave a wolf whistle. Wendy looked
up and saw Ellen parading toward the house from the
car, followed by Mother. Eric looked at Ellen, too,
and began to laugh. Wendy almost did, too. Ellen was
always in costume but today's was sillier than usual.
She had on skimpy black vinyl shorts with suspenders
and a bib, black cowboy boots with white stitching,
and a black felt cowboy hat below which dangled big
plastic earrings in the shape of guns.

"That's my hat," Chick said. "Hey, that's my hat."

"Stop looking at me that way," Ellen said to Wendy.
"Oh, what do you know anyway!" She pushed
Wendy out of the way and clomped indoors.

"Don't laugh at her," Mother said to them all.
"You'll make her feel bad."

"*I* wasn't laughing," Wendy said.

"She's crazy," Chick said. "What's she dress funny
for if she doesn't wanna get laughed at?"

Mother sighed and sank onto the back steps. Gray
pouches showed under her lovely green eyes in the
morning sun and gray hairs gleamed among the dark

ones. "She's heading straight for trouble," Mother whispered to Wendy. "And I don't know how to stop her."

"You did stop her," Wendy said. "You got her to come home instead of going to the lake, didn't you?"

"But I can't keep an eye on her every minute." Mother stood up. "I better try reasoning with her some more."

*

Later Wendy went to see if she could find Honor in the development, but Honor wasn't around. Mother was straightening up the living room when Wendy got back. "Ellen's locked herself in her room and won't come out until you apologize to her."

"Me?" Wendy asked. "What did I do?"

"She says you laughed at her."

"But I didn't."

"She's jealous of you, Wendy. She claims I favor you."

Wendy was still convinced it was the other way around, but all she said was, "Why should I apologize for something I didn't do?"

Mother looked depressed. "Please," she said. "Can't you just do it for my sake?"

"All right," Wendy said, "I'll talk to Ellen if you lie down."

Mother said she didn't have time, but added, "Thanks, darling. I knew I could count on you."

Wendy climbed back upstairs and knocked on Ellen's door. "Ell, do you hear me? I'm sorry."

"Who said you could call me Ell? My name's Ellen."

"Well, okay. I'm sorry, Ellen."

"I wish I was dead," Ellen said.

"Don't say that."

"I hate everybody in this house."

"Well, nobody hates you back." Much, Wendy
muttered to herself and to prove it she asked, "Want
to play a game with me?"

"No! Go away and leave me alone!"

Having done what she could for her mother, Wendy
was glad to oblige.

*

Sunday at noontime, Wendy called Ingrid who said
yes, she'd come to the party Saturday if Jeremy defi-
nitely wasn't coming. "Did you have a nice time with
Sarah and Marcy yesterday?" Wendy asked.

"We went to Marcy's house. She invited some boys
over. It was okay."

Wendy was encouraged enough by Ingrid's lack of
enthusiasm to ask, "How about we go hiking this
afternoon?"

"I can't. Sundays are just for the family, Mother
says."

"Oh." A silence interrupted their converation. As
usual, Ingrid left it for Wendy to fill. Ingrid made
being the talker hard because she often seemed bored
no matter how interesting Wendy tried to be. Finally
Wendy related how the boys had gotten glue on Tink
and bathed him. Ingrid laughed at that story, and

Wendy hung up satisfied with her success. It was too bad Ingrid wasn't more like Honor who listened with her eyes. Honor never made her feel boring.

*

Later that afternoon Wally was busy fertilizing the lawn. Ellen was sulking in her room. Chick and Eric had dug out last year's water pistols and were shooting water at each other from behind the bushes.

Wendy sat basking in the sun, mentally rehearsing how she'd disinvite Jeremy. She dreaded the task. Telling a lie, even a white lie, or rather a sort of gray one, made her feel squirmy. She could write Jeremy a letter with the truth—that Ingrid wouldn't come if he did—but that would be blaming Ingrid, which wouldn't be honorable. Wendy even waylaid Mother to ask for advice.

"If you've already invited him, I'd say you have to let him come."

"But then Ingrid won't."

"Well, if she won't, she won't, Wendy. You can't *make* her be your friend."

Wendy mulled it over all the way to school Monday, and the more she thought about how Jeremy was wrecking her party, the more annoyed with him she got. It just wasn't fair that she should have to suffer for his sake when he wasn't a friend of hers.

Once in homeroom, she made up her mind to hit him with the truth. She marched herself up to his desk and said, "Jeremy, about my party Saturday? I'm sorry, but you can't come."

"Why not?"

"Because . . . I can't explain it. It would hurt your feelings."

"But you already hurt my feelings."

He did look a lot like a kicked puppy as he stared at her wide-eyed. Guiltily, she looked away from him and repeated, "I'm sorry."

"It's not fair," he said. "I already told my mother and we bought you a present."

"I guess you'll have to take it back," Wendy said.

"No," he mumbled. "That's okay. I'll bring it to school and you can have it anyway."

She shook her head. The last thing she wanted was presents from Jeremy. He began fussing with his messy book bag, taking out hunks of paper and muttering to himself in an agitated way. Since he had stopped paying attention to her, Wendy slunk off to her own desk, relieved that the unpleasant task was over.

Homeroom began officially. They pledged allegiance, and Miss Pinelli talked about the track and field day in June and asked who from their class was going to enter the events. Most of the boys except Jeremy raised their hands and half the girls, including Ingrid, of course. Honor and Wendy didn't raise their hands. Honor was passing out a slip about a P.T.O. meeting. She stopped at Wendy's desk and asked, "Do you know what Germy's crying about?"

"He's crying?"

"I think so."

Wendy felt like something that should be stepped on. She looked at Ingrid. "I disinvited Jeremy," she said.

"You what?" Honor said as if she hadn't heard right.

All day Honor avoided Wendy as if Wendy had some nasty disease. Ingrid was her normal self, but she was staying for track and field practice after school and so couldn't walk home with Wendy. Walking home alone that day was lonely, until to Wendy's surprise, Honor caught up with her.

"Do you really think that little blond kid is worth it?"

"Worth what?"

"Doing that to Jeremy."

"He asked me first if he could come to my party. I didn't ask him."

"Then you shouldn't have said he could come. Once you said he could come, you were stuck with him."

"Honor, you're telling me what to do again."

"I don't care. Someone has to."

"But he isn't even a friend of mine."

"I don't know why anybody should be a friend of yours if that's the kind of person you are."

"What kind of a person?"

"The kind that can't be trusted."

Wendy shivered. Weakly, she defended himself. "Honor, you don't have a right to talk to me that way. I don't go around telling you how to behave."

"I can't help it. You don't know what it feels like to get dumped, but I do."

"Who dumped you?" Wendy asked.

"My mother when she married a man who didn't want me."

"What do you mean he didn't want you? How could anyone not want *you*? You're the best student. You behave yourself. Why, I bet you even keep your room neat."

"Sure, but I'm black, and he's white and so are his kids, and they didn't want me in their family."

Wendy was confused. "But I don't understand. Why wouldn't they want you when they want your mother? She's black too, isn't she?"

Honor huffed in disgust. "You don't have to understand about me. Just do something about Jeremy." Then Honor, whose pace was always deliberate, strode on ahead so fast Wendy would have had a hard time catching up with her.

Wendy tried to imagine how she'd feel if Wally hadn't wanted her and Mother had married him anyway. Awful. Sick. No wonder Honor was so touchy. But it wasn't the same thing with Jeremy. Wendy wasn't his mother. She wasn't even his friend.

Wendy argued with herself all the way home. Once there, she went to her bedroom to think. In the mirror her mouth hung down like a stretched rubber band. Her eyes were squinched and her curls were in the usual snarl. She looked bad. She felt bad. She'd never been especially pretty or talented or smart, but she'd liked herself for being nice. Well, she wasn't nice. Honor was right. And now what?

That evening Wendy finally got around to calling Marcy and Sarah to invite them to her party on Saturday. She wasn't surprised when first Marcy and then Sarah made an excuse for not coming. The way Wendy felt about herself, she'd be surprised if anybody came.

11

Sister Ellen

It was Tuesday morning and Ellen was still holed up in her room. Yesterday Wally had said they should ignore her until she gave up and came out. "She'll want to go to school eventually," he'd said, "even if it's just to see her friends." This morning he told Mother "Look, I'd take a day off and deal with her if I were any better at it than you, but I'm not."

"She barely touched the dinner I took up to her last night," Mother said anxiously. "She wouldn't starve herself to death, would she?"

Mother was looking at Wally, but Wendy answered, "She might."

"That's crazy," Wally said. "Tell her if she hasn't eaten by the time I get home tonight, I'm carting her off to the nut house. Tell her I mean it." Wally yanked his tie into place and finished his last sip of coffee.

"You tell her," Mother said. She backed against the refrigerator and folded her arms stubbornly.

"Right, I will."

He stomped up the stairs. Mother looked uneasy as

she listened to Wally's threatening footsteps. "I feel sort of sorry for Ellen," Wendy said, "even if it is her own fault."

"Me too," Mother admitted. "She's got to be really unhappy to keep this up, but it'd be wrong to just give in to her."

Wally was still upstairs talking to Ellen when Chick and Eric skidded through the kitchen on their way to school. They grabbed the lunch boxes Mother had filled for them, and Eric halted long enough to ask, "Can I take some of the flowers we got out back to my teacher?"

"The irises?" Mother said. "That's a lovely idea, Eric. Use the garden shears to cut them and share them with Chick."

"I'm not giving my teacher flowers," Chick said. "He's a man."

"Men like flowers too," Mother said.

"Well, *I'm* not doing it."

"Leave half of them for me for my birthday, Eric, please," Wendy put in quickly.

"Sure," Eric said before the kitchen door banged shut behind them.

"You and the boys are getting along better, aren't you?" Mother asked.

Wendy nodded. "Yeah, I think so. They're not bad kids. Eric's even sweet sometimes. . . . Mother?"

"What?"

"I did something I'm ashamed of."

Mother looked alarmed. "What did you do?"

"I disinvited Jeremy from the party."

"Oh," Mother said as if she were relieved it was nothing worse. "Well, you'll get over feeling bad."

"I'm afraid Jeremy won't though. But Ingrid wouldn't have come if he'd come, and the party wouldn't be any good without her."

"Well," Mother said thoughtfully. "Could you make it up to him somehow? Let's see. You could invite him to something else."

"I'm sure he wouldn't come after what I did to him."

"But at least it would show you *do* like him and that might make him feel better."

Wendy was considering the suggestion when she glanced at the kitchen clock. "Oh oh! I'm late." She raced upstairs, finished dressing, and sped off to school on her bike. On the way, she decided to ask Jeremy to come over to play. If he snubbed her, that was a fair punishment for what she'd done to him, and the invitation might make him feel better as Mother had said.

Miss Pinelli frowned but didn't send her to the office for a late pass when Wendy walked into homeroom. Ingrid frowned at her, too, and said, "You forgot to brush your hair."

As soon as reading started, Wendy asked to be excused and went to the girls' room to do her hair. Only she didn't have her brush in her purse, just a lot of loose tissues, a wallet with nothing but Meg's picture in it, and a button from a winter sweater. Her plaid skirt didn't match the flowered blouse she'd snatched from the closet either. Mother would have winced if she'd seen the combination.

Wendy studied the messy-looking girl she saw in the mirror. No wonder Ingrid seemed reluctant to become her best friend. The only improvement Wendy could think of then and there was to comb her hair with her fingers and turn the blouse inside out so the flowers wouldn't show. It was hard to button that way.

By the time she returned to class, the period was half over and Jeremy had been sent to the office for bopping around the room, bothering other kids who were trying to read. The first chance Wendy had to talk to him was recess. Since he was hanging upside down from the parallel bars, she spoke directly to his bellybutton.

"Jeremy, I was wondering. You know it's a girls' party Saturday, but I was wondering. Do you want to come over to my house to play on Sunday? We could have fun in the playground. It's behind my house in Honor's development. I mean, you like playgrounds, don't you?"

"You want me to come Sunday?"

"Yes, if you can."

"I'd like to come, sure. If you're sure you want me."

"Oh, I'm sure," Wendy said. "I'll save you some cake from the party. And candy." She'd give him her own share of everything. He deserved it for making it so easy for her to redeem herself.

"Did you ever look at the world upside down,

Wendy? It looks weird," Jeremy said.

"I'll bet." She walked away quickly, afraid of finding herself hanging upside down next to Jeremy like two opossums in a zoo. He certainly didn't sound angry at her for what she'd done to him. She wished the girls she knew were as easy to get along with as Jeremy.

Ingrid said she had a music lesson and couldn't go home with Wendy that afternoon.

"I didn't know you took music lessons," Wendy said.

"The organist in our church is giving them. Mother's going to clean house for her once a month in exchange for my lessons."

"Your mother must really love you to do that," Wendy said.

"I guess so," Ingrid agreed, "but I'd much rather play baseball."

The house was empty when Wendy got home, or at least she thought it was. Mother had left a note on the refrigerator for her. "Eric chipped a tooth. Took boys to dentist, Love, Mom."

Wendy had a glass of milk and a few crackers spread with peanut butter. She was licking the peanut butter off the third cracker when Ellen walked into the room. For once Ellen had no makeup on and was wearing ordinary pants and a T-shirt. "I didn't know you were home," Wendy said.

"I'm out of my room. So Dad can't cart me off to the psycho ward now," Ellen said.

"Ellen, you're pretty!" Wendy exclaimed. She couldn't remember ever seeing Ellen's face undisguised by makeup before this.

"No, I'm not."

"But you are. You look just like my mother, only younger."

"I do?"

Wendy nodded and Ellen dropped into a seat across the table from her and threw her arms wide in a gesture of despair. "Did you ever hate yourself and want to die, Wendy?"

"This morning I hated myself. Not enough to want to die though."

"You? Little Miss Sunshine? You hated yourself? I can't believe it," Ellen said. "How come?"

"I did something mean to someone. But he forgave me luckily."

"So you have a boyfriend now?"

"No. He's just a friend. I mean—" Wendy considered. Was Jeremy even a friend? "Well, a sort of a friend."

"It's so important to have a boyfriend," Ellen observed. "At my age you can't believe how important it is. Because other girls look up to you, especially if the guy's older."

"Jeremy's my age, and he's kind of—goofy. People would laugh at me if they thought he was my boyfriend."

"I can't stand being laughed at," Ellen confided. "It drives me wild."

"I wasn't laughing at you last weekend when you were dressed like a cowgirl."

"Maybe you weren't," Ellen said. "But I was so mad that I couldn't see straight. . . . your mother's not as nice as I thought, Wendy."

"You mean because she doesn't let you have your way all the time? Parents aren't supposed to."

"My mother did. My mother let me do anything I wanted before she ran away to be a stunt pilot and got herself killed."

"Do you still miss her, Ellen?"

"I hardly even remember her. I was only six. My aunt is the one I lived with most, but she never liked me much."

"My mother likes you."

"Well, she's still not going to tell me what to do. She's not my parent, really."

"Sure she is, and you don't know how hard it is for her to be strict."

Ellen rested her chin on her hand. "I hate it when people try to boss me around. It's not as if I don't know right from wrong. After all, I'm very mature for my age."

That surprised Wendy until she considered Ellen must mean she was physically mature. "Right," Wendy said. "You could get pregnant."

Ellen stared at her. "What a thing to say!"

"Well, it's true, isn't it?"

"I don't do anything with my boyfriend. All he does is kiss me."

Wendy shrugged and asked, "Want some peanut butter crackers?"

"Make me one with jelly on it," Ellen said. She hunched over the table again and started talking about her boyfriend while Wendy prepared the cracker. "He's not that tall for a high school boy, but he's taller than me, and he's not good looking, but not bad, either. I guess what I really like about him is *he* believes I'll be a star someday."

"I hope you are," Wendy said and handed Ellen the cracker. "It'd be fun to turn on the TV and see you . . . if you got really famous, they might even interview me about what you were like as a kid."

"And you'd tell them I was awful."

"No, I wouldn't," Wendy said. "You're my family." To keep the conversation going, she asked, "Are you ever going to get married and have kids, Ellen?"

"Never!" Ellen said. "I couldn't stand getting fat, even for nine months. I bet you want to get married and have kids though, don't you?"

"Sure," Wendy said. "I'd like to have lots and lots of babies."

Ellen was laughing about that when Mother walked into the kitchen with Eric and Chick behind her. "Hi," Mother said, sounding surprised. "What are you two up to?"

"Just talking," Ellen said. She hesitated, then added, "I'm sorry I gave you a hard time over the weekend, Mother."

Mother looked stunned.

"Would it be okay if I made dinner tonight?" Wendy asked. "I could cook spaghetti."

"I'll help," Ellen offered.

"You're going to cook together?" Chick asked as if he couldn't believe it.

"Go watch TV or something," Ellen told him, sounding more like her old self. "It's just girls in the kitchen tonight." Obediently, the rest of the family dispersed.

Cooking dinner with Ellen was not a treat. Everything had to be done Ellen's way. Nevertheless, since this was an historic occasion, Wendy kept her mouth shut and allowed Ellen to direct her.

*

It was such a good week, the week before the birthday party. Ingrid spent two afternoons at Wendy's house, and another day Mother and Ellen and Wendy went shopping together. Fortunately, Ellen deferred to Mother's fashion sense, so Wendy didn't come home with a bizarre outfit for the party, but she did get pants and a top that looked very good on her.

Ellen even asked what she wanted for a gift. When Wendy couldn't think of anything, Ellen decided on jewelry. She liked what she bought so well that she showed it to Wendy immediately instead of waiting for her birthday.

"I didn't think you'd want anything flashy," Ellen said, "and this matches your eyes." It was cornflower blue wooden beads with a blue bracelet to match. "Do you like it?"

"Oh yes," Wendy said. Her tears convinced Ellen that she did like the present. Actually, it wasn't the jewelry that touched Wendy, so much as that Ellen had given her something. "Thanks a lot," Wendy said and kissed Ellen's cheek.

Ellen looked startled. Then she shrugged and said, "The set was on sale anyway."

Wendy wore the necklace and bracelet to school on Friday. Honor said, "That's pretty. I didn't know you liked jewelry."

"Ellen gave it to me."

"You don't say! Wow!" Honor said with instant understanding.

"I sure hope it doesn't rain tomorrow," Wendy said.

"I think it's supposed to," Ingrid said.

"Don't worry; it won't," Honor pronounced.

It didn't, either.

12

The Birthday Party

Honor arrived at the party first wearing a colorful new top and a flower in her hair. She said thanks to Wendy's instant compliment and handed over a small package wrapped in pink and blue paper. "Happy birthday."

Wendy shook the package. "Is it a book?"

"Two paperbacks. There's one by Virginia Hamilton because you said you were interested, and one's about a cat. I never read it, but the cat on the cover looks just like Tink." Honor noticed Tinkerboy sleeping stretched flat across the back of a chair and went to pet him.

"We'll do the miniature golf first," Wendy explained, "and then come back here to eat. Chick and Eric are coming too because Ellen's visiting a girlfriend and there's nobody to baby-sit them. I hope you don't mind."

"I don't mind so long as they behave," Honor said. Tink jumped from the chair and went to the kitchen where he meowed to be let out. Mother, who was at the sink, took care of that. Honor perched on the couch to wait.

"Jeremy's coming over tomorrow," Wendy said.

"I know. He told me you invited him to go to the playground. Did he give you the gift he got you yet?"

"No."

"Well, if he remembers to bring it, act like you like it because he's really proud of it. He picked it himself. It's a flower that squirts water at people."

Wendy laughed. "That's Jeremy!" Honor laughed with her.

The doorbell rang. Wendy jumped to open the front door. Ingrid stood there in a fluffy blue party dress and white shoes with a strap and white socks. She carried a present wrapped in pink tissue paper.

"You look beautiful," Wendy said. She hoped Ingrid's fussy skirt wasn't going to get in the way of the golf stick.

With both her guests present, Wendy opened her gifts. She thanked Honor for the books and said she'd read the Virginia Hamilton one first and was sure she'd like it. Ingrid's gift was a model of a horse. It looked a little fake and plastic, but Wendy thanked Ingrid and said she would stand it on her dresser, that it was just what she wanted.

Mother appeared dangling car keys. "Ready to go miniature golfing, girls? The boys are in the car waiting. I'm sorry about having to take them along. I tried to get a baby-sitter, but no luck."

"Chick and Eric are fun," Ingrid assured Mother.

"And if they're not, there's more of us than there is

of them. So watch out, boys," Honor said sassily.

The fussy skirt didn't interfere with Ingrid's golf swing at all. She went first and sent the ball flying down the fake grass, under the bridge and into the putting green on the other side. She came in under par on the first three holes.

Honor knocked her ball over the railing with her first hit and had to chase between a teenage boy and his girl to retrieve it. She came back flustered and Wendy couldn't help but giggle. One look at Wendy and Honor started giggling too.

Then it was Wendy's turn. Giddily, she swung at the ball and missed, swung again and missed. Eric and Chick began giving her advice.

"Be quiet; you'll make her nervous," Mother said.

"Keep your eye on it and hit it, Wendy. Come on, it's your birthday," Honor coached.

Wendy swatted at the ball, keeping her eye on it. It hit the side of the covered bridge and plunked down to roll under just far enough to be beyond reach. Wendy and Honor broke into hysterical laughter.

"We're holding people up," Ingrid pointed out.

Chick wriggled under the low bridge and brought back the ball. "*You* hit it," Wendy told him. "Get it up on the green for me."

Her actual count they decided, after she'd finally managed to put the ball in the hole, was about ten over par. However, according to the rules, the worst score you could get was three over par.

"I told you I'd beat you for worst, Honor," Wendy said.

Ingrid's triumph came at the old mill stream where she got her ball into the right bucket of the waterwheel and made a hole in one. Chick and Eric did about average. Mother had settled onto a bench and was hand finishing a blouse while they played.

Wendy was winning for worst, but Honor said she couldn't be worst on her birthday. So Honor deliberately messed up by trying to hit the ball standing backward. She looked so teddy bear funny that Wendy complained, "If you don't stop clowning, I'm going to wet my pants from laughing so hard."

"Wendy! Ladies don't talk like that," Honor said with pretended shock.

Pantomiming being a lady at her next turn, Wendy minced up in make-believe high heels, fluttering her lashes. "I'm going to tap this itty bitty ball right on in," she said. Amazingly she did. That broke her and Honor up completely, and they laughed so hard they were in no shape to even try the next hole which was a hard one with an angle and a ramp. Even Ingrid came in one over par. Wendy gave up and Honor lost her ball over the fence.

Going home in the car, Honor started talking about how she and Wendy should become professional golfers. "Because talent like ours shouldn't be wasted. We could do the circuit together, Palm Beach, California, all the best places."

Ingrid was very quiet amid all the stillness. It occurred to Wendy that maybe Ingrid felt left out. To include her in the conversation, Wendy asked, "Did you play golf in Iowa, Ingrid?"

Ingrid nodded. "Sometimes my brothers took me to town and we played." She sounded wistful.

"What do you hear from them?"

"They're okay," Ingrid said. "I write them every night, but letters aren't the same thing."

"I know," Wendy said thinking of the one postcard she'd had from Meg.

Wendy said Eric and Chick could join them for the cake and ice cream since they had been so good for the first part of the party. She blew out the candles on her cake in one puff, but she forgot to make a wish.

The cake was chocolate with white frosting, pink candles, and roses the purply blue of the irises on the table. Mother had bought it instead of baking it herself, but it was good anyway. There were little tea sandwiches too, and soda and ice cream. Wendy didn't need to save her portion for Jeremy. When she had explained that she needed some for him tomorrow, Mother set aside enough of everything so that Wendy could have a mini party with Jeremy on Sunday.

Ingrid's mother came to call for her early. Ingrid stood up immediately and said, "Thank you. I had a lovely time."

"You have an ice cream mustache," Honor informed Wendy with a smile when Wendy returned from walking Ingrid to the door.

Wendy wiped her mouth and smiled back, but it didn't seem as humorous as being so bad at miniature golf had. "I don't think Ingrid had that good a time," Wendy said.

"Ingrid's boring," Honor said.

"You said that before, but I don't think so."

"Anyway, she's a good ball player," Honor conceded.

Wendy thought of all the things she could say in Ingrid's defense, like that she was brave and beautiful, but Ingrid really didn't need defending. Besides, she *was* slightly boring. "Do you have to go home, Honor? We could play a game still," Wendy said.

"Like what kind of a game?"

Wendy started naming all the board games in the house.

"How about cards?" Honor said. "We could play Old Maid with the boys if they want."

"Yeah," Chick and Eric said at the same time. They ran to get the cards.

"You want to have Jeremy all to yourself in the playground tomorrow?" Honor asked.

"Oh, no. I'd rather you'd come too if you're not busy."

"Want to bet that Jeremy will be more fun than Ingrid was?" Honor said.

"He'll be different anyway," Wendy said.

All in all she was satisfied with the way her birthday party had turned out. Ingrid may not have had that great a time, but then Wendy couldn't think of an occasion when Ingrid had ever really seemed to be joyful. Honor had had fun and so had Wendy. Leftover laughter was still fizzing inside her after Honor went home.

13

Friends

Wendy stared out the window and anxiously chewed on the end of a curl. The silver streamers of spring rain were so dense that it seemed impossible there could be any sun up there above them.

"What's the matter with you?" Ellen asked. She was basting together a sundress that Mother had cut out for her.

"Jeremy's not an indoor kid. He can't sit still for long. I was counting on the playground and now it's too wet."

"Hyperactive people get on my nerves," Ellen said. "When's he due?"

"Now. It's one. I told him any time after one was fine."

"I think I'll go sew in my room," Ellen said and instructed Wendy, "You don't have to bother introducing me." It took her two trips to move her sewing plus her Walkman upstairs.

Eric bounded into the room a minute later. "Did your friend come yet?"

"Not yet."

"Well, when he comes, can I play with you guys?"

"Where's Chick?"

"He's mad at me because I squashed his worm."

"Still? You did that this morning."

"Well, he says it was a special worm. He says maybe it was magic."

Wendy smiled. "Okay, you can play with us—when he gets here. If he comes." Jeremy, being Jeremy, might very well not come. He could have gotten the day wrong, or have lost her address, or the person who was supposed to drop him off might have changed his mind. She had just given up on him and settled down to read Honor's birthday book when the doorbell rang.

Jeremy wasn't even wearing a raincoat. "I forgot your present, and my brother-in-law wouldn't let me go back and get it."

"That's okay. Come on in; you're getting wet."

Wendy introduced him to Eric who immediately asked if Jeremy wanted to play with the race car set. "Sure," Jeremy said. While Eric ran upstairs to get his set, Jeremy examined the living room. "This is a nice house," he said. He sat in the biggest armchair, then bounced on the couch which he left so that he could examine the rocker by the window. Wendy was reminded of Goldilocks and the three bears.

"Maybe I should call Honor up and invite her over

here," Wendy said. "She was supposed to meet us in the playground, but we can't go in the rain."

"Sure," Jeremy said. "I like Honor."

He followed Wendy into the kitchen where she introduced him to Wally who was cutting ads out of the paper. "What are you doing that for?" Jeremy asked. Wally explained his mower had broken down and he was looking for another used one.

"You don't need to," Jeremy said. "My brother could fix the one you got. He can fix anything. I bet he'll do it for free because Wendy's my friend."

"Well, thanks," Wally said. "But the truth is I'd like a newer model than I've got."

"What's better about a newer model?" Jeremy asked.

During Wally's description of lawn mower gadgetry, Wendy called Honor who said she was in the middle of Sunday dinner but would come over as soon as she could.

Eric appeared in the living room lugging a box as big as he was. "Hey, want to help me set the tracks up?" Eric asked Jeremy.

"Sure," Jeremy said. "Wow, that's some set. These are neat cars. Wow!"

He and Eric got so busy laying out the tracks on the carpet, making sure they were level and that the curves were angled right, that they forgot Wendy was in the room.

She went back to her reading. When she looked up at the end of a chapter, she discovered Chick had wordlessly inserted himself into the race car activity.

All three boys were intent on their project. Half an hour later she realized that the whizzing noise of the cars had stopped. The boys were on their way upstairs. "We're going to play alien invaders and earthmen," Jeremy said over the railing. "Want to come?"

"No, thanks. Not unless you need me." Since they kept going up to Chick and Eric's room, she assumed they didn't. Entertaining Jeremy was a lot easier than she'd expected.

The phone rang. "It's for you," Wally said. "Listen, Wendy, your mother's due home from that fashion show in a couple of hours. I'm going to go check out some of these ads. That okay with you?"

"Fine," Wendy said.

The phone call was from Honor who wanted to know if she was coming to the playground. "It's stopped raining," Honor said.

"Everything'll be wet."

"I'll bring an old towel. How's Jeremy doing over there?"

"No problem," Wendy said. "He's playing with my brothers."

"You don't want to come?"

"Well, I could use some fresh air. I'll ask him."

Jeremy said sure, he'd come. Chick and Eric promptly tagged along. Even Tinkerboy decided to join them at the last minute.

"Is that your cat?" Jeremy asked when Tink emerged from under a bush, as dry as if he'd been indoors all the time.

"Yes, that's Tinkerboy."

"I recognized him from the composition you wrote last fall. You write good compositions, Wendy."

"Thank you," Wendy said with pleasure. She was amazed that something she'd written would stick in Jeremy's head for almost a year. Either she was a better writer or he had a better memory than she'd imagined. Tink followed behind them across the backyard.

Honor was drying off all the swings with a large blue bath towel that had a hole in the middle. "I did the big slide by going down it on the towel," she said.

"This is a neat playground," Jeremy said. He promptly headed for the railroad tie mountain. Eric, Chick, and Tink followed him.

Wendy and Honor chose adjacent swings.

"Jeremy's the easiest person I ever entertained," Wendy said.

Honor laughed. "I see what you mean."

For a few minutes everything was peaceful. Wendy and Honor stared up at the sky where gussets of blue showed between gray drifty cloud. Swinging made all the cloud activity above speed up in an interesting way. Wendy leaned her head way back and let the wind tumble her hair.

"Uh oh," Honor said. "Here comes that kid again."

"What kid?"

"The bully. I forget his name."

Wendy looked. "Everett," she said and dragged her toes to stop the swing. She watched the square, tough-looking boy climbing to the top of the mountain where Jeremy was perched by himself. Chick and Eric were on the seesaw now.

"Move," Everett told Jeremy.

"Sure," Jeremy said agreeably. He scrambled down the mountain and went over to the seesaw. "Hey, Chick and Eric, bet I can lift both of you at the same time."

"Bet you can't," Chick said. He was right. Jeremy was too skinny.

"Let me. I can do it," Everett said.

"No. I'm going on the slide," Chick said. Eric followed him up the ladder, and Jeremy brought up the rear. Immediately, Everett went to kneel at the bottom of the slide and block it with his body.

"You can't come down until I say so," Everett said with a sly grin.

"Watch out, you; here I come," Chick said. He aimed his basketball sneakers right at Everett's face.

Everett twisted away from the slide, slipped, and landed in the mud. "I'm going to get you for that," he said. He started after Chick, but Chick was too fast. Chick and Eric and Jeremy raced off through the project with Everett in pursuit. Meanwhile Tink climbed to the vacated top of the mountain and sat there surveying the world.

"Rats," Wendy said. "I knew it couldn't be easy if Jeremy was involved."

"But it's not his fault," Honor said. "It's your brother's."

"Anyway, I better get help and my parents aren't home. What should I do, Honor?"

"Grab the boys and hide out in my apartment. Only my grandma won't be too thrilled if three messy boys come tromping over her cream-colored carpet. Also, she hates noise."

Chick was in the lead as the boys appeared, having run clear around one section of the apartment complex. Next came Eric and then Jeremy. Everett wasn't more than an arm's length behind Jeremy. "Uh oh," Wendy said. "I better go do something." She trotted toward the runners. Honor stayed right beside her.

"Okay, you, Everett," Wendy said. "Why are you chasing those kids? They were playing nice until you came along."

"You the counselor here or something?" Everett sneered.

"No, but I'm telling you, you better leave those kids alone."

"Or else what?"

Wendy couldn't think of an "or else," but behind her, Honor said, "Or else there's five of us and only one of you, and you'll be sorry."

Everett considered that. While he was considering, Jeremy and Chick and Eric joined ranks with Honor and Wendy so that Everett did find himself facing a battery of five. "I don't like being pushed in the mud," he said.

"You weren't pushed; you fell," Wendy told him.

"It was an accident," Jeremy said.

"It was your own fault," Honor pointed out boldly.

Everett looked around him as if seeking reinforcement. Not finding any, he shrugged. "Okay," he said. "I'll let you guys off this time. But you better stay out of this playground. You don't belong here anyway."

"I do," Honor said, "and they're my friends. And what apartment do you live in?"

Everett frowned and growled something under his breath.

Tink announced his presence with a *mrrowl* and rubbed past Jeremy's legs to Wendy.

"Whose cat is that?" Everett asked.

"Mine," Wendy said. Before she could bend to pick Tink up, Everett swooped down and scooped Tink up by the fur on the back of his neck. Then he turned and ran with an outraged Tink swinging from his fingers.

Wendy howled and gave chase. She had the whole gang with her. Back through the playground ran Everett, holding the yowling cat at arm's length. He stopped at the mud puddle in front of the swing set and tossed Tink into the middle. By then everybody had stopped running except Jeremy, who rammed into Everett. Unbelievably, Everett teetered and fell again, right into the mud puddle which Tink had instantly vacated.

"You big jerk," Jeremy yelled. "That's what you get for being mean to animals."

Without another word, they all turned and raced for Wendy's house. Tink reached the yard first.

"I hate bullies," Jeremy said when they were safely inside. "They make me so mad."

"You really stood up to that kid, Jeremy," Wendy said. "You were terrific."

"I was?"

"Yes, you were," Honor said.

"I bet Tink thinks so too," Wendy said.

"We should've beat that kid up after you knocked him down," Chick said.

"No. It's not fair to hit somebody when they're down," Jeremy said. He sounded so adult that Wendy looked to make sure it was him talking. It was, and he looked pleased with himself.

"Let's do something quiet," Honor said. "We've had enough excitement for one afternoon."

"Yeah," Chick said, "it was *fun*."

"Jeremy, do you want your cake now?" Wendy asked.

"No, thanks. I'm not supposed to eat sweets. My mother says it makes me hyper."

"Not ice cream either?"

"No, but I could drink a glass of water."

There were potato chips in the pantry. Jeremy ate those with his water while the rest of them shared the party food Wendy had saved for him.

Jeremy's ride came for him then. "Bye, you guys. I gotta go," he yelled. "It was a good party." He sounded as if he meant it, too.

Honor excused herself to go home next, and Chick and Eric disappeared up to their room again. Tink meowed outside the living room window. Wendy let him in to soothe and pet him. He was a little damp but free of mud.

"Where's your father?" Mother asked, coming in all dressed up from the fashion show she'd attended at the mall.

"Shopping for a lawn mower," Wendy said.

"And Ellen?"

"Upstairs."

"You mean you had to entertain that boy all by yourself?"

"Eric and Chick entertained him mostly. And Honor. It was easy," Wendy said. "Actually, I think Jeremy's more normal out of school than in." She was too tired to go into a long explanation about Everett and Tink.

"That's a relief," Mother said. "I was a little worried about what you'd gotten into by inviting him today."

"It was a fun weekend," Wendy said.

In fact, if she didn't examine it too carefully, she could even imagine she'd been surrounded by friends. Of course that wasn't actually the case. Ingrid was a slipping away friend. Honor, despite what she'd said to Everett, wouldn't declare herself a friend. Jeremy was a misfit of a friend. As to Chick and Eric and Ellen, they were family.

One good thing was that Wendy liked herself again now that she'd made things right with Jeremy. The only problem was that she still didn't have what she wanted most, what she should have wished for yesterday when she blew out her birthday cake candles and forgot to make a wish. Too bad she'd missed her chance.

She went upstairs to write Meg about her birthday weekend.

14

The Best Friend

On Monday, Wendy went to school eager to see her companions of the weekend and found herself strangely isolated. Honor was out sick. As for Jeremy, Mrs. Hunt had finally given him the time on the computer that he'd been begging for, and he was spending great chunks of class time in the media center working on what he called his "Crazy Quiz." He claimed it would be useful as an option for kids who didn't want to compete in athletic events on track and field day.

Ingrid was in class, but when Wendy asked her how her Sunday with the family had gone, she said only, "It was okay." Then Wendy started telling her about the adventure with Tink and the bully, and in the middle of it Ingrid said, "Excuse me, I have to talk to someone." She walked across the room to where Marcy and Sarah were giggling together. Sarah immediately made room for Ingrid to sit beside her.

It hurt Wendy to see Ingrid's flyaway blond head

bent close to Marcy and Sarah's for a private exchange. It hurt when Ingrid sat with them at lunch and Wendy was left alone at the other end of the table. But the worst hurt was when Ingrid claimed to be busy after school every day that week. Either she had organized activities to attend or she was just "busy." Now that the project on early man was complete, they weren't working in groups anymore, either. Ingrid had become as distant as if she were sitting on the opposite side of the room instead of right next to Wendy.

Wendy wondered what she'd done wrong that Ingrid didn't seem to like her anymore, but she felt shy about asking, and by midweek she'd decided not to. She was afraid to hear that Ingrid never had liked her much, and finally she admitted to herself that she'd suspected it all along.

*

Friday Miss Pinelli called Wendy up to her desk and asked her privately if she'd bring Honor some of her books and assignments to do at home. "The nurse says Honor's not sick herself," Miss Pinelli assured Wendy. "Her grandmother has a bad back and Honor's staying home to take care of her."

Happy to have an excuse for visiting Honor, Wendy rushed home, snacked on cookies, told her mother where she was going, and set off with Honor's books and papers in hand. A rosebush was blooming in the back of the yard. Wendy backtracked to ask if she might bring the flowers to Honor's grandmother.

"Lovely idea," Mother said. "I like Honor. She's livelier than that other friend of yours, the little blond one."

"Ingrid. Ingrid's not my friend anymore, Mother, and as for Honor, she isn't either."

"Why not, puss?"

"I told you," Wendy said. "Lately nobody seems to like me much."

"I'm sure that's not true," Mother said staunchly and added what she'd said before, "How could anyone not like you!"

Comforting as Mother's loyalty was, it didn't cast much light on the matter, but Wendy was grateful for it anyway.

"*I* think you're okay too," Ellen threw in. She breezed past them and out the kitchen door without even pausing for a reaction.

"Ellen's late for her voice class," Mother said. The corners of her lips twitched. Then she and Wendy were laughing together because, as Mother said, "From Ellen, 'okay' is high praise."

The roses were small and grew in clusters. By cutting off a few branches, Wendy had a full bouquet of flat, frilly red flowers that were cheery if not particularly graceful. Lugging both books and flowers, she set off to locate Honor's apartment. The silky spring air had brought out young mothers with their toddlers who were making full use of the baby swings and small slides in the playground.

Honor had an upstairs apartment in a cluster near

the road. Wendy rang the bell beside the outside door and waited on the stoop. Feet clumped on the stairs. Then Honor's voice asked, "Who's there?"

"It's me. Wendy."

Honor opened the door looking suprised.

"Miss Pinelli sent me," Wendy said. She asked, "How's your grandmother?"

"Still flat on her back. She says I have to go to school next week and she'll manage alone, but I don't see how."

"Can't you hire a nurse?"

"Too expensive, and all Grandma has to do is lie still, so she doesn't need much besides meals and a bedpan. A lady from the Girls' Home where Grandma works comes by after work to help her bathe."

"It must be boring for you," Wendy said.

"A little. After three days of reading, I'm about read out."

"I could go to the library if you need more books."

"No, thanks. I can get away for that." Honor accepted the paper bag with her school materials and thanked Wendy for bringing them.

"I thought your grandmother might like some flowers," Wendy said and proferred the bouquet.

Honor stared at the flowers without taking them.

"They're just from my garden," Wendy explained.

"I know . . . I was just thinking . . . how about if you come upstairs and give them to her yourself?"

"Okay," Wendy said.

Pleased by the unexpected invitation, she followed

Honor up the green carpeted steps to the second floor apartment. They stepped into a foyer. Across from it was a closet-sized kitchen lined with modern appliances and cupboards. Beyond that was a sunny alcove full of big plants around a dinette table and chairs. Wendy glanced to her left and saw the cream-colored living room carpet Honor had mentioned once. The furniture looked formal, and fancier than the battered, homely pieces in Wally's house. Honor led the way down a narrow hall where three doors opened to two bedrooms and a bathroom.

"Grandma," Honor said, blocking the doorway so that Wendy couldn't see inside the bedroom. "Somebody brought you flowers. You want to say hello?"

"Why isn't that nice! I certainly do," the grandmother said cordially.

Honor stepped aside to let Wendy in. Suddenly Wendy got nervous about chatting with Honor's formidable grandmother, but she offered up a big smile and said, "Hi." Honor's grandmother looked harmless enough lying in bed covered by a flowered quilt. "I was bringing Honor her school work, and I thought you might like these roses from our garden while I was at it."

The grandmother's mouth was still set at welcome, but her eyes showed dismay. Wendy was obviously not someone she wanted to see. However, the grandmother said pleasantly, "That's very kind. Thank you. Honor, get that tall vase down from the closet, will you?"

Elderly people, in Wendy's experience, appreciated

concern about their ailments. So she asked, "Does your back hurt even when you're lying down?"

"Not if I stay still. I told Honor not to stay home from school for my sake, but she wouldn't listen. Missing school's a sacrifice for her. She's one child who really loves school."

"That's because she's so smart," Wendy said. She and the grandmother exchanged small smiles. Wendy relaxed a little. She noticed the wall of framed photographs next to the grandmother's bed and asked, "Oh, may I look at the pictures?" Permission granted, Wendy circled around the bed to stand close to the wall. "Which one is Honor's father?"

"The tall boy there. That's my favorite picture of him. It's when he graduated from high school."

The slim, dark-skinned young man in the picture was smiling broadly as he stood with his hands on his hips, ready to take on the world. "He's handsome. Honor has his eyes, doesn't she?" Wendy asked. "Was he a good student too?"

"No," the grandmother said. "She gets that more from me. My son was so good natured that everybody liked him, but he was no student."

Without further prompting from Wendy, the grandmother continued proudly showing off her gallery of family protraits. She pointed out the large black man who looked as grim as the grandmother had the first time Wendy saw her. "That was my husband. He was my history teacher in high school, ten years my senior and the finest man I ever knew."

"The high school here in town?"

"That's right. I grew up in a house across from the high school. My son and I only moved here after my husband died. There's Honor with her father."

The photograph showed a chubby little girl in a white party dress and white shoes sitting on her father's knee. It looked as if another figure had been in the picture and had been cut out because Wendy could see an arm around Honor. The arm was white. Wendy stared at it. To whom had the arm belonged? The figures were in a typical family pose. She remembered Mother asking if Honor's mother was black, and just because Honor and her grandmother were black, Wendy had assumed the mother had to be too. Not so, it seemed. Honor's mother was white, or at least her arm was. No wonder Honor was so complicated.

"It's sad that your son died," Wendy said to the grandmother.

"They're all dead except for Honor and me." The grandmother's voice was so heavy with sorrow that Wendy ached in sympathy.

The glass vase squeaked as Honor slid it along the dresser top. "Would you like some fudge, Wendy?" Honor asked. "I made Grandma and me some chocolate fudge yesterday."

"Yes, thank you," Wendy said.

"Come on to the kitchen then. You need anything right now, Grandma?"

"No," the grandmother said. "You go ahead and enjoy yourselves. And then why don't you go out and get some fresh air? It'd do you good."

"Want to go for a walk or something, Wendy?" Honor asked.

"Yes, let's," Wendy said.

The fudge was so delicious that Wendy had two pieces. "I make it with butter and beat it a long time," Honor explained.

Downstairs Honor asked where Wendy wanted to walk and Wendy said, "We could go to the country."

"But I only have about an hour. I've got to get back for the lady that helps Grandma bathe," Honor said.

"An hour's enough," Wendy said. "I'm talking about the field on the other side of the highway. Mother and I call that the country."

"Oh, there," Honor said. "Yes, that's a good idea."

Honor ambled along, sniffing the air and looking around dreamily. Wendy asked her, "How come you let me meet your grandmother?"

"Just taking a chance. I couldn't believe how she liked you. And you, you were really something the way you knew how to say all the right things."

"What things?"

"Oh, about my father and grandfather and me being smart. All you forgot to mention was the cream-colored carpet. Next time you can tell her how much you like that." Honor laughed and Wendy laughed with her, barely able to believe what she thought she was hearing.

"And she liked me?" Wendy asked to hear it again.

"Sure, couldn't you tell? I was practically holding my breath because if she hadn't, it would have been ugly."

"So why did you take the chance then?"

"Just to show her, I guess. I don't know. Grandma doesn't trust white people. Most of them. She says when push comes to shove they let you down, even the ones that seem nice at first."

"I'd never let you down, Honor."

"Well, who knows. You let Jeremy down."

Wendy bit her lip. What could she say? "Yes, that was bad," she admitted.

"Well, but," Honor said quickly, "you tried to fix it. You care about people. You have a good heart."

"Thanks," Wendy said, "I'm glad you like something about me anyway."

"Oh, I've *always* liked you. I just didn't want—see, when I lived with my mother, even after my father died and Mother and I were living alone, I had mostly white friends, some black, but my best friend was white."

"Is your mother white, Honor?"

"Yes, she sure is. Didn't I ever tell you that?"

"No. I just guessed from that picture, the one with you on your father's knee."

"Oh . . . yeah. Grandma cut Mama out of the picture. Grandma was so mad that she wanted to marry that man anyway, even though I'd told Mama what his kids said—you know, about not wanting me."

"Didn't your mother believe you?"

"She believed me. She just said his kids would change their minds once they had a chance to get to know me. I told her I wasn't giving them a chance if they were ignorant enough to hate me because I'm black. They said they were going to make my life miserable. They said ... awful things. I begged my mother not to marry him, but you know what she said? She said, 'You'll grow up and leave me, Honor, and I need someone who'll stay.'"

"She didn't make you go to live with your grandmother?"

"Not really. I did that to punish her because—well, she knows my grandma hates her and tried to keep my daddy from marrying her."

"And now you don't see her any more?"

"Sure I see her. We talk on the phone like once a week, or more if I have a problem. And she takes me out on my birthdays, and last year when his kids were in camp, I stayed with Mama and him for a week."

"Do you like your stepfather?"

Honor shrugged. "He's okay ... I still love my mother a lot even though I'm mad at her, and Grandma doesn't want me to have anything to do with her. 'Stick with your own kind and you won't get hurt,' Grandma says."

"But your own kind's both black and white."

"Not according to Grandma. She says I'm black, not half and half. She says if you've got black blood, the white world treats you as if you're all black, and so you better accept it and be proud of it. Grandma says being black makes you beautiful and strong and deep. Closer to God, too."

"Then you can't have a white friend?" Wendy asked and held her breath.

"I told you what my grandmother thinks," Honor

said. "That doesn't mean I think it, too."

Wendy looked at Honor's face. "Well then?" Wendy asked hopefully, but they'd reached the highway.

"Hurry up," Honor said.

They ran across the two lanes and entered the field past a fringe of cattails in the ditch. Wendy pointed to ferns unfurling green fists amid the grasses. They crouched next to each other to study them. "I love buds and things when they're new and opening up," Wendy said.

"Umm," Honor agreed. "Me too."

Thinking of Honor, Wendy said, "I'd die if I had to leave my mother."

"You wouldn't have to leave her. You're not like me. Your mother and you are both the same color."

"Are you a color or a person, Honor?" Wendy asked impatiently.

Honor blinked and looked soft in her surprise. She said, "Sometimes I'm not sure."

"To me you're a person," Wendy told her, "a super person. I wish you'd be my friend, Honor."

"But I'm not really the kind you want," Honor said. "All that business you wrote about being alike as two peas in a pod and hanging on the phone every night and wearing the same clothes and calling each other secret names—I don't go for that kind of junk."

Wendy winced, recalling her composition on friendship and Meg. It seemed a little childish now.

"The way I look at it," Honor continued earnestly,

"you don't wind yourself around a friend like a strangler vine, and you don't expect friendship to be always and forever."

"But Honor, if it doesn't last, what good is it?"

"I didn't say it *wouldn't* last. All I'm saying is, we shouldn't expect it to because life's sure to change us, you and me. In high school, we'll be different people, and boys will come in the picture—for you anyway. I don't know if I'll have time for them if I'm going to be a lawyer. And if boys don't do us in, then after high school we'll go our separate ways, and that'll make it hard."

"Honor, what you're saying!" Wendy said gleefully.

"What?"

"That we *are* friends now."

Honor frowned and admitted, "Well, I need *someone* to talk to, and you're the best listener around."

She sounded so grouchy about it that Wendy had to grin. For a while she walked in silence, enjoying the soft tickle of pleasure in her chest. They arrived at the stagnant pond where the fields stopped and woods began, and a red-winged blackbird dipped past them, flashing its chevrons. Suddenly Wendy felt triumphant. Without half trying, just by being herself mainly, she'd won Honor's friendship. It had come like a gift, an unexpected gift, a prize she had won. Maybe that was how friendship should come.

"I better be getting back," Honor said.

"Let's run then."

"Me run? Are you crazy?" Honor said, but Wendy

grabbed her hand and they began running in wild, awkward abandon back through the lemony twilight. Around them was the mysterious zinging and peeping of small night creatures. Ahead of them was the long, free summer. They ran, and Wendy was filled with joy as she pulled her new best friend through the soft night of the country and across the highway toward the bright lights of home.

WORLDS OF WONDER
FROM
AVON CAMELOT

THE INDIAN IN THE CUPBOARD
Lynne Reid Banks 60012-9/$3.99US/$4.99Can

THE RETURN OF THE INDIAN
Lynne Reid Banks   70284-3/$3.50US only

THE SECRET OF THE INDIAN
Lynne Reid Banks   71040-4/$3.99US only

BEHIND THE ATTIC WALL
Sylvia Cassedy   69843-9/$3.99US/$4.99Can

ALWAYS AND FOREVER FRIENDS
C.S. Adler   70687-3/$3.50US/$4.25Can